HARLEQUIN®
Presents

Happy New Year! Have you made any resolutions for 2007?

The editors of Harlequin Presents books have made their resolution: to continue doing their very best to bring you the ultimate in emotional excitement every month during the coming year—stories that totally deliver on compelling characters, dramatic story lines, fabulous foreign settings, intense feelings and sizzling sensuality!

January gets us off to a good start with the best selection of international heroes—two Italian playboys, two gorgeous Greek tycoons, a French count, a debonair Brit, a passionate Spaniard and a handsome Aussie. Yummy!

We also have the crème de la crème of authors from around the world: Michelle Reid, Trish Morey, Sarah Morgan, Melanie Milburne, Sara Craven, Margaret Mayo, Helen Brooks and Annie West, who debuts with her very first novel, *A Mistress for the Taking.*

Join us again next month for more of your favorites, including Penny Jordan, Lucy Monroe and Carole Mortimer—seduction and passion are guaranteed!

We're delighted to announce that

A Mediterranean Marriage

is taking place in
Harlequin Presents®—
and you are invited!

Imagine blue skies, an azure sea, a beautiful
landscape and the hot sun. What a perfect place
to get married! But although all ends well for
these couples, their route to happiness is filled
with emotion and passion. Follow their journey
in the latest book from this inviting miniseries.

Sarah Morgan

BLACKMAILED BY DIAMONDS, BOUND BY MARRIAGE

A Mediterranean Marriage

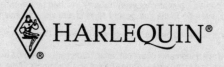

HARLEQUIN®

TORONTO • NEW YORK • LONDON
AMSTERDAM • PARIS • SYDNEY • HAMBURG
STOCKHOLM • ATHENS • TOKYO • MILAN • MADRID
PRAGUE • WARSAW • BUDAPEST • AUCKLAND

ISBN-13: 978-0-373-12598-2
ISBN-10: 0-373-12598-4

BLACKMAILED BY DIAMONDS, BOUND BY MARRIAGE

First North American Publication 2007.

This edition published by arrangement with Harlequin Books S.A.

www.eHarlequin.com

Printed in U.S.A.

All about the author...
Sarah Morgan

SARAH MORGAN was born in Wiltshire and started writing at the age of eight when she produced an autobiography of her hamster.

At the age of eighteen she traveled to London to train as a nurse in one of London's top teaching hospitals, and she describes what happened in those years as extremely happy and definitely censored! She worked in a number of areas in the hospital after she qualified.

Over time her writing interests had moved on from hamsters to men, and she started creating romance fiction. Her first completed manuscript, written after the birth of her first child, was rejected by Harlequin, but the comments were encouraging, so she tried again; on the third attempt her manuscript *Worth the Risk* was accepted unchanged. She describes receiving the acceptance letter as one of the best moments of her life, after meeting her husband and having her two children.

Sarah still works part-time in a health-related industry and spends the rest of the time with her family trying to squeeze in writing whenever she can. She is an enthusiastic skier and walker, and loves outdoor life.

CHAPTER ONE

THE UNMISTAKABLE SOUND of footsteps echoed around the ancient stone stairs that led to the basement of the museum.

Angie Littlewood glanced up from the notes she was making, distracted by the unexpected disturbance. Upstairs the museum was heaving with visitors but down here in the bowels of the old listed building there was an almost reverential silence, a silence created by thick stone walls and the academic purpose of the researchers and scientists who worked behind the scenes.

Angie felt a flicker of surprise as she saw Helen Knightly appear in the doorway. As Museum Curator, Helen was usually fully occupied upstairs with the public at this time of day and Angie's surprise turned to consternation as she saw the distressed expression on her colleague's face.

'Are you all right, Helen? Is something the matter?'

'I don't know how to tell you this, dear.' Helen's face was slightly paler than usual and Angie's heart took an uncomfortable dive as her mind raced ahead, anticipating the problem.

Obviously it was something to do with her mother. Gaynor Littlewood had been so traumatized by the events of the last six months that Angie was sometimes afraid to leave her alone in the house.

'What's happened?'

'There's someone upstairs asking to see you.'

With an inward sigh, Angie carefully replaced the piece of ancient pottery she'd been examining and rose to her feet, still holding her pen. 'If it's my mother again, then I apologise,' she said huskily, adjusting her glasses and her white coat as she walked towards the curator. 'She's found the last six months very hard and I do keep explaining that she can't just turn up here unannounced—'

'It's not your mother.' The curator gave a nervous cough, a gesture that did nothing to ease Angie's growing feeling of unease.

If it wasn't her mother then it had to be a funding issue. Research posts were always precarious and money was always in short supply. She felt a sudden stab of panic. *How would they manage without the money from her job?* Angie opened her mouth to prompt the other woman but the heavy tread of male footsteps on the stairs distracted her.

She glanced towards the door as a man strolled into the room without waiting for either invitation or introduction.

For a brief moment Angie stared at him, her attention caught by the strength and perfection of his coldly handsome face. He resembled one of the legendary Greek gods, she thought, her mind wandering as she studied the perfect bone structure, the masculine jaw and the hard, athletic physique. All the Greek myths she'd ever read rushed through her head and for an extremely unsettling moment she imagined him stripped to the waist, bronzed muscles glistening with the sweat of physical exertion as he did battle with the Minotaur or some other threatening creature while some hapless female lay in chains on the floor waiting to be rescued.

'Dr Littlewood? *Angie!*' Helen's tone was sharp enough to disturb Angie's vision and she gave herself a mental shake, reminding herself that sponsors didn't expect archaeologists to be dreamy. And this man was obviously someone extremely important. He had an unmistakable air of command and authority and her eyes slid to the two men who had planted themselves in the doorway behind him. Their manner was respectful and watchful, and added to her feeling that the man was hugely influential; he was probably considering making an extremely large donation to the museum. Although she would rather be left in peace to do her research, she was only too aware that posts such as hers existed only because certain organisations or individuals were financially generous. Clearly Helen Knightly was expecting her to fly the flag and make a good impression so she pushed down her natural shyness, *ignored her deep-rooted belief that men as glamorous and sophisticated as this one never looked twice at women like her,* and stepped forward.

It didn't matter that she wasn't beautiful or elegant, she told herself firmly. She'd graduated top of her year from Oxford University. She spoke five languages fluently, including Latin and Greek, and her academic record was excellent. If he was interested in funding a position at the museum, then those were the qualities that would interest him.

'I'm very pleased to meet you.' Still holding the pen, Angie stretched out a hand and heard Helen make a distressed sound.

'Angie, this isn't—I mean, I should probably introduce you,' she began, but the man stepped forward and took the hand that Angie had extended.

'You are Miss Littlewood?' The voice was strong and faintly accented. The grip of his strong bronzed fingers matched the power of his physique. Which god did he most closely resemble? Apollo? Ares? Angie felt her mind drift again until she heard Helen's voice in the background.

'This is Nikos Kyriacou, Angie, the President of Kyriacou Investments.'

A Greek name? Given the comparisons she'd been making, Angie almost smiled and then Helen's words and the urgent emphasis of her tone finally registered.

Nikos Kyriacou.

The name hung in the air like a deep, dark threat and then reality exploded in Angie's head and she snatched her hand away from his and took an involuntary step backwards, the shock so great that the pen she was holding clattered to the floor.

She'd never heard of Kyriacou Investments but she'd heard of Nikos Kyriacou. For the last six months his name had been on her mother's lips as she'd sobbed herself to sleep each night.

Clearly aware of the sudden escalation of tension in the room, Helen cleared her throat again and gestured towards the door. 'Perhaps we should all—'

'Leave us.' His dark, brooding gaze fixed on Angie. Nikos Kyriacou issued the command without a flicker of hesitation or the faintest concession towards manners or protocol. 'I want to talk to Miss Littlewood alone.'

'But—'

'It's fine, Helen.' Angie spoke the words with difficulty. *It was far from fine.* Already she could feel her knees shaking. She didn't *want* to be left on her own with this man. The fact that he was rude came as no surprise. She'd already deduced that he was a man devoid of human decency—a man with no morals or ethics. Now she knew which Greek god he most closely resembled. *Ares,* she thought to herself. *The god of war.* Cold and handsome but bringing death and destruction.

Her slim shoulders straightened as she braced herself for conflict. This wasn't the time to be pathetic. She owed it to her family to stand up to him. The problem was, she *hated* conflict. Hadn't her sister continually mocked her because

Angie always chose the peaceful route? The only argument that interested her was an academic one. All she really wanted was to be left in peace with her research.

But that wasn't an option.

Staring at him now, she decided that he was every bit as cold and intimidating as his reputation suggested and suddenly all she wanted to do was run. But then she remembered her sister as a child, so blonde and perfect, always smiling. And she remembered her mother's limp, sobbing form—remembered all the things she'd resolved to say to Nikos Kyriacou if she ever met him face to face.

Why should she be afraid of being alone with him? What could he do to her family that he hadn't already done?

His dark, disturbing gaze remained fixed on her face as he waited for the echo of Helen's footsteps to recede.

He had nerve, she had to give him that. To be able to look her in the eye and not appear to feel even the slightest shred of remorse.

Only when he was sure that Helen Knightly had moved out of earshot did he speak. 'First, I wish to offer my condolences on the death of your sister.'

His directness shocked her almost as much as the hypocrisy of his statement. The words might have meant more had they been spoken with the slightest softening of the voice but his tone was hard. The coldness injected into that statement somehow turned sympathy to insult.

She inhaled sharply and pain lanced through her body. 'Your condolences?' Her mouth was so dry she could barely speak the words. 'Next time you're offering your condolences, at least try and look as though you mean it. In the circumstances, your sympathy is rather out of place, don't you think? In fact, I think you have a complete nerve coming here and offering "condolences" after what you did!' It was the first time she'd ever spoken to anyone in such a way and she reached out a hand and held on to the table, needing the support.

A frown touched his proud, handsome face, as if he were unaccustomed to being questioned or criticised. 'Your sister's death at my villa was extremely unfortunate, but—'

'Extremely unfortunate?' She, who never raised her voice, who always preferred logic and reasoned argument to mindless aggression, raised it now. A vision of her sister flew into her mind. *The sister she'd never be able to hug and laugh with again.* 'Unfortunate? Is that how you justify it to yourself, Mr Kyriacou? Is that how you appease your conscience? How you manage to sleep at night…'

Something dangerous flared in those dark eyes. 'I have no trouble sleeping at night.'

She was suddenly aware of her pounding heartbeat and the dampness of her palms. An instinctive urge of violent aggression swarmed through her and she must have betrayed that urge in some way because the two men in the doorway suddenly stepped forward, ready to intervene.

Angie realised that she'd actually forgotten their presence. 'Who are they?'

'My security team.' Nikos Kyriacou dismissed them with an impatient gesture and they melted into the background, leaving Angie alone with the one man in the world she would have preferred never to meet in person.

'I can understand why a man like you would need a security team if you treat everyone the way you treated my sister! Clearly you have no conscience!' She placed both hands on her desk. It was that or punch him hard. 'My sister died in a fall from your balcony and you're standing there telling me that your conscience is clear?'

Fine lines of tension appeared around his hard, sculpted mouth. 'There was a full police investigation and a post mortem. The verdict was accidental death.' His flat, factual statement held not a trace of emotion and her anger rose to dangerous levels. She'd had no idea that she was capable of feeling such undiluted fury. It was because she hadn't been given the chance to express her feelings, she told herself. She'd been so busy caring for her mother. It was only at night when she was given the chance to stop and think and then her head was crowded with thoughts of her sister. Her little sister. *The person she'd loved most in the world.*

Tears stung her eyes and she blinked them away. 'Accidental death. Of course. What else?' She couldn't keep the sarcasm out of her voice. 'You're a very important person, are you not, Mr Kyriacou?'

His powerful body stilled. 'I'm not sure what you're implying, Miss Littlewood, but I should warn you to be careful.'

There was something in his tone that made her shiver although she didn't understand exactly what because he still hadn't raised his voice or displayed anything other than the utmost control.

She remembered reading a business article that had described Nikos Kyriacou as cold, ruthless and intimidating and suddenly she could understand why a journalist might have come to that conclusion. His unsmiling, icy calm was in direct contrast to her boiling emotions.

Normally she would also have described herself as calm but she was fast discovering that grief did funny things to a person. She was discovering parts of her personality that she hadn't been aware existed—basic urges that had never before revealed themselves—*like the desire to wipe that superior expression from his indecently handsome face.*

'It's *Dr* Littlewood.' She lifted her chin and corrected him in the tone she reserved for the most arrogant students that she lectured at the university. 'And you don't frighten me.'

'Doctor, of course. Dr Angelina Littlewood. And the purpose of my visit is not to scare you.' He gave a faint smile that implied that if he'd wanted to frighten her it would have been an easy task. She curled her fingers into her palms.

'I don't use the name Angelina.' In her opinion it was a ridiculous name. A name suited to an entirely different sort of woman—a beautiful, glamorous woman, not a studious, plain archaeologist. 'I prefer to be called Angie, as you would be aware if you knew the first thing about me.'

His hard gaze didn't shift from her face. 'I know a great deal about you. You have a diploma in classical archaeology, a PhD in Mediterranean archaeology and you specialise in the art and pottery of the classical Greeks. Quite an impressive academic record for someone as young as you. Tell me, *Dr Littlewood*—' his gentle emphasis on her title was impossible to ignore '—do you often find it necessary to hide behind your qualifications?'

Still recovering from the shock of discovering that he knew so much about her, Angie tightened her grip on the desk. 'Only when I believe I'm being patronised.'

'Is that what you think?' He studied her closely, his eyes sweeping the white coat, the glasses and the fiery hair tortured into a neat coil at the back of her head. 'You're nothing like your sister, are you?'

Intentionally or not, he had used the weapon designed to create the most serious wound.

She turned away then, unwilling to reveal the agony that his words caused. She knew she was nothing like Tiffany— had long ago accepted that they were entirely different in virtually every way. But those differences hadn't affected the bond they'd shared. Even as Tiffany had moved from caring child to wayward, moody teenager, Angie had still loved her deeply. Knowing that they had little in common had done nothing to ease the pain of her sister's death. If anything it made it slightly worse because Angie felt a continuous gnawing guilt that she hadn't tried harder to influence her younger sister. *To persuade her to modify her behaviour.* And that guilt wasn't helped by her mother's constant obsession with 'what if's. What if Angie hadn't been so disapproving of Tiffany's desire for fun? What if Angie hadn't been so boring and obsessed with work? What if she'd flown out to Greece and kept Tiffany company? What if she'd been with her sister the night of the accident?

Tortured by those recurring thoughts, Angie raised a hand and rubbed at her brow, trying to relieve the ache. She was almost beginning to believe that she'd played a part in Tiffany's death—by allowing her sister to continue down the path of self-destruction. By not trying to keep her away from men like Nikos Kyriacou.

'Did you read the report?' Cold and relentless, his voice continued to torment her and she turned, understanding the full meaning of his question without needing elaboration.

'If you're asking me whether I knew she was drunk, then the answer is yes,' she said quietly, noting the flash of surprise in his eyes. 'What? Did you think I didn't know? Or did you think I'd deny that knowledge?'

'Since you evidently hold me responsible for the accident despite the fact that the report completely absolved my family of blame or responsibility, I thought the facts might have escaped you.'

She stared at him in disbelief. 'The facts are that Tiffany was young, Mr Kyriacou. She celebrated her eighteenth birthday just two months before she started working in one of your hotels. Most eighteen-year-olds have been drunk at some point or another; it's part of the passage into adulthood.'

'Have you, Dr Littlewood?'

She frowned. 'I fail to see the relevance of that question.'

'Really?' He gave a faint smile, so maddeningly calm and detached that she wondered for a moment if he was a lawyer by training. He seemed to be trying to trap her into saying something that would absolve him of responsibility.

'If you're suggesting that Tiffany's slightly inebriated state in any way exonerates you of blame then I'm afraid I don't see it that way. I find your complete indifference nothing short of insulting given the circumstances. *You* were the reason she drank that night! It was *all* your fault!'

Why had she always avoided confrontation in the past? It was actually remarkably liberating being able to say exactly what she thought.

Apparently unmoved by her accusations, Nikos raised a dark eyebrow in sardonic appraisal. 'You think I held the bottle to her lips?'

'I think you might as well have done. In normal circumstances you and my sister would never have crossed paths but unfortunately fate threw you together.'

'Fate?' The heavy sarcasm in his voice goaded her still further. She didn't know what he was implying but it was clearly something derogatory.

'My sister was a waitress! She had a two-year contract with your hotel! Her only role at jet-set parties was pouring champagne into the glasses of people like you!' Her voice echoed round the stone walls of the museum and she took a deep breath and forced herself to lower her voice. There had already been more than enough gossip surrounding her family. She didn't need more. 'Tiffany was young and starry eyed and you took advantage of that. You were *totally* out of her league, Mr Kyriacou, and you should have recognised that even if she didn't. You should have stuck to models and actresses and other women who understand the rules of the games you choose to play. But you just couldn't resist my sister, could you?' Her voice rang with contempt. 'You took advantage of her innocence and broke her heart.'

There was a long, tense silence. A silence during which he studied her face with a disturbing degree of concentration. 'It is not my wish to defame your sister's character,' he breathed, 'but clearly we have a significantly different interpretation of events and also of your sister's personality.'

'Of course we have! How else would you be able to live comfortably with your conscience? You've clearly managed to persuade yourself that you were totally without blame. But the truth is that Tiffany had never even had a proper boyfriend until she went to Greece and yet you—' She broke off, hot colour flooding her cheeks and he tilted his proud, handsome head in question.

'—and yet I?' His prompt was lethally soft. 'Please don't hold back on my account, Dr Littlewood. Please enlighten me as to my behaviour towards your innocent sister. I confess I'm fascinated by your alternative view on the world. Clearly you've spent a significant proportion of your life closeted in the depths of museums and universities.'

Why, she wondered in silent amazement, did women find him so attractive? Was it the air of danger? The sense of menace? It was like confronting a tiger with sheathed claws, knowing that it would take little for him to display his deadly power.

True, he was extraordinarily handsome but he had an icy, remote quality that made her shiver.

Angie thought of all the things that her mother had said about Nikos Kyriacou. Thought of the file of pictures she'd kept on the man. The fact that her mother had been proud of her sister's new romantic attachment had filled Angie with horror and frustration.

'The man is at least fifteen years older than her,' she'd pointed out, but her mother had merely shrugged dismissively.

'He's *loaded,* Angie, not to mention influential. Whatever happens now, she's made. Being with him will give her access to circles that she never would have had a chance of entering if she hadn't been on his arm. They say he has billions—that he's absolutely brilliant at business. So clever. He's dated supermodels and actresses, but never for more than a few weeks at a time because apparently he has no intention of ever marrying. And yet he's been seeing our Tiffany for at least six weeks! It's obviously serious. Can you believe that?'

She'd had great trouble believing it. 'Why would a man like Nikos Kyriacou be interested in Tiffany?' If he were truly as clever as rumour suggested, then Tiffany, whose conversational skills didn't extend beyond fashion and hairstyles, would surely have bored him in minutes. She'd loved her sister, but love hadn't blinded her to the truth.

Her mother had bristled at the question. 'Tiffany is extremely pretty,' she'd said defensively, 'and a traditional Greek male values beauty in a woman, not brains. I don't expect you to understand because your idea of a good night is having your nose stuck in some big fat book with long words in a foreign language, but when a man comes home from a hard day making millions he's hoping for something a little more stimulating than conversation. Not that you'd know anything about that.'

Angie had given a murmur of derision, wondering why it was that brilliant men turned into idiots when confronted by a pretty face. She'd seen it with her father. Clearly Nikos Kyriacou suffered from the same lack of restraint when it came to women. Her mother was right. It was something that she didn't understand and never would.

Looking at him now, there was no doubt in her mind where

the responsibility for her sister's death lay. 'Tiffany was very innocent. At the very worst she was perhaps a little foolish.'

'You think so?'

She thought she detected a dangerous flash of fire in his dark eyes but it vanished in an instant and he appeared as controlled as ever. Unlike her. She felt the last strands of control slipping from her grasp. Telling herself that it was impossible to appeal to the conscience of a man who clearly didn't possess one, Angie launched a powerful defence of her sister.

'You're supposed to be a sophisticated man of the world. I can't believe you couldn't see what was beneath the blonde hair and make-up. I can't believe you didn't know the truth about her.'

'I knew all about her,' he said flatly, a tiny muscle flickering in his lean cheek, 'but I'm starting to wonder whether you did.'

'I know my sister always dressed and acted in a way that suggested that she was far older than she actually was. But she was a child. She didn't play by your rules and you must have known that! You should never have made false promises.'

He inhaled sharply and his eyes narrowed. 'What promises am I supposed to have made?'

Angie shook her head, unable to believe that even he had the gall to deny what he'd done. 'You vowed to marry her and we both know that would never have happened. It's well documented that marriage never appears on your agenda.'

There was a long, tense silence. 'What makes you think I promised to marry her?'

'Because she told me! I'm sure you were hoping that she'd kept your proposal a secret. How very inconvenient for you that she didn't!' Her hands shaking, Angie reached for her bag and rummaged inside for her mobile phone. 'She sent me a text two weeks before she died. *Two weeks before she fell from your balcony,* Mr Kyriacou.'

He was unnaturally still. 'Show me.'

She scrolled down through the texts and stopped when she reached 'Tiffy'. The name brought a lump to her throat. 'It says: "N going to marry me. So happy!" She was alive when she sent that text—' She thrust the phone into his hand and swallowed hard. *She wasn't going to cry.* 'She was in love with you and she was *happy.* The next text was sent the night she fell. Read it, why don't you?'

"'Just discovered truth about N. Hate him.'" He read the words aloud, staring at the phone in his hand, his tension visible. 'So it was true then. She did expect marriage,' he breathed and Angie gave a humourless laugh.

'And why would that come as a shock to you? Because she should have known better than to believe you when you promised to marry her? Tiff was a young girl and like all young girls her head was full of romance and happy endings. You ought to remember that next time you contemplate having some fun with a teenage girl. She was no match for a man like you and you broke her heart! Presumably that was why she was drunk that night. She'd discovered the sort of man you really are!'

Something dangerous flared in his eyes. 'You know nothing about the sort of man I am, Dr Littlewood.'

'I know that my sister shouldn't have been anywhere near you! Every time I open a newspaper you're with another woman.' *A beautiful, glamorous woman.* 'It's obvious that you see the female sex as entertainment and nothing more.'

The tension in his powerful frame increased significantly. 'And you always believe what you read in newspapers?'

'Not all the detail, of course not. I'm not stupid. But the stories have to come from somewhere.'

'Is that right?'

'Which brings us back to the question of what a man like you was doing with a girl like Tiffany.'

'I'm sure you'll tell me, given that you know so much about me from such a reliable source.' There was a biting edge to his tone that made her stiffen.

'Don't play games with me and don't ever joke about my sister's death!'

'Believe me, I don't consider anything about your sister to be funny, least of all her death.' There was something about his excessive stillness that made her increasingly uneasy and suddenly the fight drained out of her and she just wanted him to leave.

She sank on to her chair and rubbed her hands over the fabric of her plain, practical navy trousers. 'Please go.' Her voice was husky and she removed her glasses and looked up at him. 'I don't know why you came here, but I want you to leave now. And I want you to promise not to go anywhere near my mother.'

That cold gaze rested on her face and a faint frown touched his dark, sculpted brows. 'Why do you wear glasses?'

'I'm sorry?' The irrelevance of the question threw her and she blinked in astonishment as she stared up at him. She noticed for the first time that his lashes were very thick and very dark and softened the otherwise hard lines of his handsome face. 'I need them for very close work, for seeing detail, but I don't understand why you—'

'You should wear contact lenses. It won't compensate for your unfortunate personality but it would at least soften your appearance and make you appear more feminine.'

She gave a gasp of outrage, just *mortified* by the personal nature of his less than flattering comment. She shouldn't care, she reminded herself. All her life her mother had been making similar comments about her appearance. Angie, wear a dress. Angie, have a haircut. Angie, wear make-up. She didn't seem to understand that dressing up wouldn't make a difference. Her eldest daughter was plain. She'd been born plain and she'd die plain. And it didn't matter to her. All that mattered at the moment was that she'd lost her little sister.

Feeling emotions that she didn't entirely understand, she immediately fumbled for her glasses and slipped them back on to her nose. 'I'm not interested in your opinion on anything, Mr Kyriacou.' Her voice trembled as much as her fingers. 'The only thing that interests me is the reason for your visit. Clearly you didn't come to apologise, so why did you come? Or do you take pleasure in viewing other people's distress? Are you one of those people who slow down on the motorway to view an accident on the opposite carriageway?'

There was a long silence while he studied her, a silence during which she grew more and more uncomfortable. Why was he looking at her like that? Was he ever going to speak?

Finally he drew breath and something in the depths of his dark eyes made her stomach flip with nerves. Instinctively she sensed that she wasn't going to like what he was about to say.

'Why did you come here?' Her voice cracked slightly and his mouth hardened.

'Have you ever heard of the Brandizi diamond?'

His question was so unexpected that she frowned. 'Why would I?'

He gave a faint smile and waved a hand around the room she worked in, gestured to the various artefacts that surrounded her. 'Because you're interested in history and legend, Dr Littlewood, and the Brandizi diamond is surrounded by both.'

'As you've already pointed out, my speciality is Greek art and pottery of the classical era. I know very little about jewellery.' She straightened her shoulders. 'I fail to understand the relevance of this conversation.'

'The Brandizi diamond is one of the most valuable stones ever documented. It is a flawless pink diamond. The exact date of the piece is unknown, but it is believed to have been commissioned by an Indian prince as a gift for his first wife as a symbol of eternal love. Apparently he believed in such things.' His faint smile of derision revealed his thoughts on that topic. 'Great superstition surrounds the diamond.'

Even though she would have walked on broken glass sooner than admit it, something in his cool, cultured tones had caught her imagination. Angie's eyes slid to the fragments of pottery that lay on her desk. 'Myth and legend are always closely aligned with ancient artefacts. Much can be learned about people's beliefs by studying the art of the time.'

'The stone came into the possession of my family several generations ago. It has traditionally been passed down to the eldest son to offer as a gift to the woman of his heart. It is of incalculable value in both monetary and emotional terms.'

Her own heart started to beat faster and she felt the rush of excitement that she always felt when discussing the past. But then she reminded herself that Nikos Kyriacou wasn't another academic and she couldn't afford the luxury of conversation with this man, however stimulating the subject.

'I fail to see what any of this has to do with my sister.'

He looked at her for a long moment and then strolled over to a cabinet and examined one of the pots on display, leaving Angie to stare at his glossy dark hair and broad shoulders with increasing frustration.

She took a deep breath and tried again. 'What does this diamond have to do with my sister?'

'Everything.' He turned then, a muscle flickering in his hard jaw, his eyes glinting Mediterranean-dark. 'Your sister was wearing the Brandizi diamond on the night she fell from my balcony, Dr Littlewood. I suspect that it was amongst her belongings when they were returned to you. And now I want it back.'

CHAPTER TWO

ANGIE stared at him in astonishment. 'My sister was wearing this rare diamond the night she died? The Brandizi diamond? The one that's worth gazillions?'

She saw the tension ripple through his powerful frame. 'That is correct.'

'The same diamond that is given by the men of your family to the women as a symbol of eternal love?' She gave a disbelieving laugh, finally appreciating the true irony of the situation. 'Did my sister know that story?'

His strong jaw was clenched. 'Very possibly.'

'So the fact that she was wearing the diamond would have supported her genuine belief that you loved her and intended to marry her, wouldn't it?'

'For a respected archaeologist, you have an alarming gift for misinterpreting the facts, Dr Littlewood,' he growled softly and she gave a humourless laugh.

'On the contrary, I think I'm just establishing the facts for the first time. Answer me a question, Mr Kyriacou. Did you love my sister?'

His hesitation answered the question. 'We had an understanding,' he said finally and she nodded.

'I'm sure you did. My sister was young and very easily

seduced by the prospect of money and romance. She would have been easy prey for a sophisticated man of your experience.'

'I refuse to discuss the circumstances of your sister's death any further,' he growled and she had some satisfaction in noticing that his icy cool had finally melted away to be replaced by simmering anger. 'All you need to know is that the diamond did *not* belong to her.'

And clearly he wanted it back.

Aware that she now had the power to make his life *extremely* uncomfortable, Angie felt a sudden rush of adrenaline. The fact that he had shown absolutely no emotion towards her sister and yet now seemed increasingly tense, merely supported her poor opinion of him. He was a man interested in money, power and possessions. Nothing more. He cared more about the loss of the diamond than he did about the loss of her sister. That, he'd made clear, was nothing more than an inconvenience for him. Had the diamond not been around her sister's neck when she'd died, Angie had absolutely no doubt that he wouldn't have bothered to make this visit and the knowledge increased her own anger. He should be *made* to care.

'But if she was wearing it the night of her death, the night she fell from your balcony, then presumably you must have given it to her. And what was it you just said?' She frowned slightly, pretending to think, drawing out the confrontation with relish. 'That it was a symbol of love, given to the "woman of your heart"? Presumably that's why Tiffany sent that text. She knew that once she was wearing the famed necklace, her future as your wife was surely secure.'

Nikos Kyriacou walked towards her, his brooding dark gaze intent on her face. 'Tell me, Dr Littlewood, when you find something of the past—' he lifted a fragment of pottery from her desk and turned it slowly in his fingers '—do you presume to immediately know its authenticity?'

She frowned. 'Of course not. We have several techniques for dating objects and for establishing use and value.'

He brushed a finger over the surface of the fragment that he still held, examining the pattern closely. 'So you would agree that something is not always as it seems? That fakes and frauds do sometimes make an appearance in this less than perfect world of ours?'

'Yes, but—'

'And, as an academic, part of your job is to explore the truth behind the facts, is it not?' He placed the fragment back on her desk with exaggerated care. 'Not to judge by appearances, as so many less informed and less educated people might?'

Reminded that her approach to life was to search for evidence before drawing conclusions, Angie felt a flash of discomfort and then reminded herself that Nikos Kyriacou was playing games with her again, manipulating her with words. He'd probably done exactly the same to her sister. According to her mother, he negotiated billion dollar deals on a regular basis so he was obviously skilled at twisting a situation to his advantage, which was clearly what he'd done with Tiffany. She had no intention of allowing him to do the same with her. It was true that she'd dealt with this whole situation in an emotional way that was completely out of character, but given the circumstances was that really so surprising? And anyway, she wasn't just judging on appearances. She *knew* Tiffany.

'My sister was in love with you. I have a text from her that indicates her sincere belief that you intended to marry her. I now discover that she was wearing your diamond—your rare and precious diamond given to the woman of your heart. And yet you try and persuade me that appearances can delude?' She rose to her feet again, so angry that she could barely speak. 'Allow me to tell you that although appearances can mislead, they can also be astonishingly accurate. Things often turn out to be *exactly* as they first seem.'

'The diamond did not belong to your sister.' His tone was a low, threatening growl and for a moment she almost imagined that she could see the dangerous claws unsheathed from those soft, deadly paws.

'And yet she died wearing it and in love with you. The facts appear to speak for themselves, wouldn't you agree?'

Clearly goaded to the limits of his patience, he inhaled sharply and proceeded to let out a stream of Greek that he incorrectly assumed she wouldn't understand.

Slightly smug that his research into her background had failed to reveal that she was fluent in his language, Angie kept her eyes on the desk and waited for him to calm down. Had he spoken in English, the words he'd used would have made her blink with shock but, as it was, the fact that he was capable of losing his temper gave her considerable satisfaction and slightly soothed her own frayed emotions. At least he was capable of feeling *something,* even if it was only anger and frustration that she was proving to be so uncooperative.

He planted both hands on her desk and fixed her with his unusually penetrating gaze. 'You must understand that the retrieval of this diamond is *extremely* important to my family.'

Should she reveal that she spoke Greek? Deciding not, Angie gave a faint smile.

'And you must understand that my sister's death is extremely important to mine.' She looked up then, her eyes glistening with tears. 'Do you notice the fundamental difference between us, Mr Kyriacou? Your focus is on objects and mine is on people. I may study ancient artefacts but those artefacts tell us a great deal about people and the way they lived, just as your desire for this diamond says a great deal about you. When you first arrived I assumed that you had come to offer explanation and seek forgiveness but now I discover that you merely wanted to collect lost property.'

There was no longer a trace of the ice cool restraint that had been so much in evidence when he'd first arrived. Instead his dark eyes flashed dangerously and his mouth hardened. He looked like a volcano on the brink of eruption. And that was a place that no sensible being would want to be.

Her legs shaking and her stomach churning, Angie picked up her bag and walked towards the door, unaccustomed to conflict and anxious to end the encounter. 'Thank you for taking the trouble to visit me personally, Mr Kyriacou. It was a most illuminating conversation.'

She battled through the rain and a tube train crowded with tourists and arrived home to find the house unusually silent. One glance at the empty sherry bottle on the kitchen table was enough to tell her how her mother had spent the day. Presumably she was now in bed, sleeping off the excess of alcohol she'd consumed.

Drained and exhausted from her confrontation with Nikos Kyriacou, Angie stripped off her wet coat and immediately made for the attic where she knew her mother had stowed the suitcase that had been returned to them from Greece. *The suitcase containing her sister's belongings.*

The attic was dusty and crammed with bits of old abandoned furniture and tattered boxes but she saw the suitcase immediately and paused with her hand on the zip, emotions churning inside her. Her mother hadn't even opened it and she couldn't blame her for that. It wasn't something she was looking forward to doing either.

Her mind went to the myth of Pandora who had been instructed not to open the box under any circumstances. Yet the temptation had proved too great and she'd released terrible forces into the world. Angie chewed her lip, unable to bring herself to open the suitcase. Would it contain something she'd wish she'd never seen? Would her life be changed?

Impatient with the ridiculous flight of her habitually over-active imagination, Angie sucked in a breath and unzipped the case. The first thing she saw as she lifted the lid was a glittery piece of fabric designed to be used as a wrap. It was so typical of her sister's flamboyant taste that she gave a faint smile. Then she put her hand in the case again and pulled out her sister's handbag. It was badly stained and Angie felt her stomach lurch. It must have been the bag she'd been holding when she'd fallen. Not allowing herself to dwell on the origin of those stains, she put the bag carefully to one side and moved the other items of clothing and then her hand stilled.

It lay in the bottom of the case, winking and catching the late evening light that poured through the small attic window. Angie caught her breath. Even with absolutely no knowledge of diamonds, she could see that the stone and the setting were exquisitely beautiful.

In a trance, she reached down and lifted the pendant from the case, feeling the weight of the stone settle into the palm of her hand.

Without warning, her eyes filled and the ache inside her was so great that she could hardly breathe. *Her sister had been wearing this on her last day alive.* It had been round her neck, had touched her skin, been part of her—

'I miss you, Tiff,' she whispered and then gave a start of shock as her mother's voice came from directly behind her.

'What's that?'

Angie blinked back the tears, cleared her throat and turned. Her mother was staring at the diamond with more animation and excitement in her expression than she'd shown for months.

'It belongs to the Kyriacou family,' Angie said immediately, closing the case with her free hand so that her mother wouldn't have to see the rest of Tiffany's belongings. 'I wasn't going to tell you, but he visited me today and asked for this back.' She deliberately revealed nothing of the stress of the encounter and her mother didn't ask. Instead her eyes were glued on the jewel in Angie's palm.

'My Tiffany had that round her neck when she died? It's the Brandizi diamond.'

Angie stared at her mother in astonishment. 'You *know* about it?'

'Of course. I've seen it round the neck of Aristotle Kyriacou's wife. Eleni, I think her name is. She doesn't often wear it in public because of its value.'

And it had been sitting in their attic unprotected. Angie felt faint at the thought. What if they'd been burgled? Not that any local burglar would have been expecting to find one of the world's most famous and valuable diamonds in the attic of a terraced house in North London. She almost laughed at the thought.

'Well…' She closed her hand around the diamond, unable to put it down. Holding it somehow gave her a connection to her dead sister. 'I have to return it to the Kyriacou family.' She said the words for her own benefit as much as her mother's. To remind herself that it was stupid to attach sentimental value to a jewel that hadn't even really belonged to her sister.

But she didn't want to give it away. They had so little of Tiffany left. The necklace was the last thing she'd worn and that made it almost a part of her.

'We should keep it.'

Angie's gaze softened with sympathy and understanding. 'Because giving it away feels like losing part of Tiffany?'

'No.' Her mother shot her an impatient glance. 'Because keeping it feels like getting our own back on the bastards.'

Angie winced. Despite years of practice, she'd never understand her mother. 'Don't be silly, Mum. It doesn't belong to us.'

Angie's gaze slid from her mother's hard expression to the glittering diamond that lay in the palm of her hand. It was hard not to remember the words that Nikos Kyriacou had spoken: *It has traditionally been passed down to offer as a gift to the woman of his heart.* And yet he clearly hadn't loved Tiffany at all.

'I can't believe my Tiffany was wearing that necklace.' Her mother's tone was reverential and Angie felt a rush of exasperation mingled with a total lack of comprehension. In her opinion, her mother had a totally misplaced sense of pride.

'Nikos Kyriacou clearly gave it to her in return for sex, Mum,' she mumbled as she stood up and negotiated her way down the ladder that led from the attic. 'I don't really think that's anything to boast about.'

'It's given by the man to the woman he intends to marry.'

Angie stopped halfway down the ladder. 'Pardon?'

'The diamond. It's given as a gift by the man to the woman he intends to marry. I read it in an interview with Kyriacou's wife. So if my Tiff had it round her neck, then that's proof that Nikos Kyriacou intended to marry her.'

'Nikos Kyriacou had no intention of marrying anyone,' Angie said wearily. 'He isn't the marrying kind. He's exactly like Dad. The sort of man who moves from one woman to another without care, thought or emotional involvement of any sort. He *never* would have married Tiffany.'

'Then he should be taught a lesson!'

'Now you're being ridiculous.' Angie reached the bottom of the ladder and helped her mother down. 'Kyriacou is a billionaire in a league of his own. According to that article you showed me a few months ago, he owns five jets, nine properties, including his own island in Greece. *His own island, Mum!*" She said the words slowly to emphasise her point. 'He's considered a genius in business, you told me that yourself. Now look at us. We live in North London in a terraced house, most of which the bank owns.'

Her mother's lip wobbled. 'It isn't my fault that your father frittered away all our money on women and then went bankrupt.'

Angie sighed. 'I know you're not to blame, Mum. All I'm saying is that we're hardly in a position to teach a man like Nikos Kyriacou a lesson, no matter how much we might like to.' *Especially when I'm just an archaeologist and you're a lush,* she thought to herself.

'We have his diamond.'

Angie frowned, failing to see the relevance of that statement. 'You're not seriously suggesting we keep it? Even if we wanted to, that wouldn't be an option. Legally, it belongs to the Kyriacou family. And they have the money to buy all the lawyers they need to reclaim it. We don't have a decent argument for keeping it.'

She had a ridiculous vision of herself standing up in court telling dark-suited lawyers that she wanted to keep the jewel because it was the last thing that had touched her sister's skin. Even *she* knew that such a sentiment would attract nothing but derision.

Her mother's eyes were suddenly hard. 'That man should be taught a lesson! He destroyed my Tiffany and he should pay! He's Greek, isn't he?' Her voice rose to a shrill pitch. 'Revenge! The only language these Greeks understand is revenge. You should know that—it's in all those stupid stories you read.'

'Myths, Mum. They're called myths.'

Her mother gave a snort of derision. 'Whatever.'

'They're stories, Mum, not real life. In real life people like us don't go round seeing revenge.' *It was time to give the doctor a call to discuss her mother's drinking.* 'I'm going to contact him and give the diamond back. It's the right thing to do. Go back to bed, Mum. I'll see you in the morning.'

Nikos lounged at the back of the lecture theatre, watching through narrowed eyes as the students poured into the room, jostling and chatting, clutching bags and computers ready for the lecture.

Without exception, all the women cast interested and hopeful glances in his direction but he ignored their lingering attention and focused his gaze at the front of the room.

He was waiting for Dr Littlewood.

Their encounter the previous day had left him angrier and more frustrated than he could ever remember feeling.

It wasn't that he'd ever expected the meeting to be an easy one. He hadn't. It was more that he was unaccustomed to finding himself questioned or challenged and Angie Littlewood had done both.

In fact she'd goaded him to such a degree that he'd been on the point of revealing the entire truth about her sister and only monumental self-discipline had prevented him from doing anything so foolish. For a start, it was obvious that Angie Littlewood approved of her sister's behaviour but, most importantly, revealing the truth risked bringing nothing but misery on his family. If Angelina Littlewood took the story to the press then the whole distasteful, sordid mess would be exposed. *And that had happened once before with disastrous consequences—*

A horrifying vision flashed into his brain and he dismissed it with ruthless determination. *It wasn't going to happen again,* he promised himself. He was going to prevent it. This time he was in control of the situation and he had every intention of remaining in control.

Once the Brandizi diamond was back in his possession, the whole ugly chapter could be closed. His contact with the Littlewood family would be over and, as far as he was concerned, that moment couldn't come soon enough. It was true that the two sisters were entirely different but the elder was every bit as unappealing as the younger, albeit for different reasons.

And, right now, she was late for her own lecture.

As a man who valued and practised punctuality, he was contemplating the clock on the wall with brooding disapproval when the door opened and Angie Littlewood hurried in, juggling a pile of files, wisps of hair escaping from the clip at the back of her head.

She looked flustered and out of breath and he noticed that her hand was shaking as she stepped up to the lectern and switched on the microphone. 'I apologise for being slightly late—' Her voice had a smoky, feminine quality that dragged across Nikos's nerve-endings and sent a stab of elemental lust through his loins.

Irritated and surprised by the strength of his reaction, Nikos shifted in his seat in an attempt to ease the insistent throb of his body. Exactly *why* he should suddenly experience such a powerful reaction to a woman like Angie Littlewood escaped him. She was so far removed from his usual choice of companion that it was laughable. He was used to women who revelled in their femininity whereas Dr Littlewood seemed totally unaware, even indifferent, to the possibilities of her sex. She was wearing a plain roll-neck top under her jacket and the same plain navy blue trousers that she'd had on the previous day. It was the attire of a woman who dressed for practicality and convenience rather than allure.

If he hadn't already established her relationship with Tiffany, he would never have believed that they were sisters.

And yet there were similarities, he mused, his eyes resting on the unmistakeably generous swell of her breasts and the

dip and curve of her tiny waist. She lifted an arm to emphasise something on a slide and he saw that her wrist was slender
and her profile remarkably delicate. Part of Tiffany's appeal
had been her external appearance of fragility and it appeared
that her sister shared that essentially feminine characteristic.

Remembering the way she'd challenged him during their
previous meeting, he gave a smile of derision. There had
been nothing fragile about the way she'd behaved. And her
defence of her sister's indefensible behaviour was nothing
short of distasteful.

Realising that the audience around him were listening with
rapt attention, he forced himself to listen to what she was
saying and found himself surprisingly absorbed in her lecture
on classical Greek pottery. *She knew her subject,* he thought
to himself as he watched her breathe life and meaning into the
past as she talked.

She had a few artefacts on the table in front of her and she
used these and her slides to illustrate her lecture. She spoke
fluently, without notes, clearly passionate about her subject,
unaware of the passage of time or the slow descent of her hair
from the clip. Each time she turned and gestured, the knot
slipped a little more until finally her hair escaped its bonds
and cascaded over her shoulders. *Amazing colour,* Nikos
thought to himself as he watched her scoop it into her hand
and continue to talk, her almost breathless enthusiasm holding
the entire auditorium in enraptured silence.

Only as she paused to draw breath did she finally glance
at the clock. 'I've run over as usual! That's it for today—I have
notes here if anyone wants them—and don't forget that there
are more examples in the museum on the second floor if you
have time to look before Friday.' Her hair slid forward over
her shoulders in a tumbled mass of fiery, flaming curls and
Nikos observed the transformation with masculine fascina-

tion. She no longer looked like a serious archaeologist. Instead she looked like—a woman?

And yet there was no doubt that she considered her hair to be nothing more than an annoyance as she reached for the clip to fasten it back from her face but was then distracted by a student who approached to ask her a question.

She immediately forgot her hair and became absorbed in the discussion. Another student approached and, by the time they reluctantly allowed her to stop talking, the rest of the lecture theatre had emptied.

He stood up and strolled down the steps towards her, watching as she reached for the files on the desk and gathered them up. Only as she turned did she finally notice Nikos standing in front of her.

'I find it hard to believe that you've suddenly developed an interest in Greek pottery of the classical era.' Her tone was brittle as she clutched the files to her chest, clearly shocked to see him. 'So I assume you're here for another reason, Mr Kyriacou.' Behind her glasses, her blue eyes seemed more luminous than ever and he found himself wanting to rip off the glasses and study her face properly.

'Let's not play games, Dr Littlewood.' Angered by an impulse that he didn't understand, he walked forward and picked up a pot that lay on the desk, turning it over in his hands. 'Very pretty. A good copy of a *psykter*—a red figured wine cooler. It would have been filled with wine and floated in ice cold water until the wine was cool enough to drink. About 500 BC?' He saw surprise in her eyes.

'You clearly paid attention in the lecture.'

'I'm Greek,' he reminded her softly, returning the pot to its place on the table. 'I'm interested in the heritage of my country. And also that of my family.' He let the words hang in the air for a moment and saw her chin lift.

'If you're referring to the necklace, then I should warn you that I haven't yet had a chance to look for it.'

'You're lying.' His eyes rested on her nose and he noticed the tiny freckles that danced over her pale skin. 'The first thing you would have done when you arrived home last night was look for it.' The faint colour that touched her cheeks told him that his assessment was accurate.

'The first thing I did when I arrived home last night was care for my mother. She is extremely unwell and has been since we received the news of Tiffany's death. Searching through my sister's belongings is a low priority.'

'In that case, give me the suitcase and I will conduct the search myself.'

Her eyes flashed with anger and contempt. 'Your schedule is of absolutely no interest to me whatsoever and if you come within a million miles of our house, Mr Kyriacou, I will call the police.'

Unaccustomed to being continually challenged, Nikos felt his frustration rise. 'I'm ordering you to give me the diamond.'

'And I don't respond to orders, especially from people I don't respect.'

Swiftly he changed tack. 'If you're thinking, even for a moment, that you can make money out of this situation then let me tell you right away that you're in for a severe disappointment. The diamond does not belong to you or your late sister. If you are planning to sell the jewel for money then it's only fair to warn you that it would prove impossible to find a buyer. The stone is so famous that no reputable dealer will touch it and its value is incalculable.'

'You *still* think this is about money?' She threw her head back and her hair poured over her shoulders like tongues of flame. 'Is that *all* you think about? How very sad your life must be!' The raw blaze of anger in her eyes caught his attention and he watched her transform in front of his eyes. From cool academic to passionate woman.

She was still dressed in the boring, sober suit but Nikos no longer noticed what she was wearing. He was transfixed by the burning fire in her unusual blue eyes and by the almost feral wildness of her hair.

Accustomed to women who existed from one blow-dry to the next, women who discouraged any activity which might disturb razor-sharp perfection, Nikos suddenly had an inexplicable desire to sink his hand into those wild fiery curls and bring his mouth down hard on hers. Just how far did that wildness of hers extend?

Seriously disturbed by the entirely inappropriate direction of his own thoughts, he took a step backwards just to make absolutely sure that he wasn't tempted to touch her. 'It isn't about money. It's about regaining something which is rightfully mine.'

'You are an insult to the human race!' She stepped off the podium and stalked towards him, her anger a live and powerful force. 'Six months ago my sister died falling from your balcony and we heard nothing from you. *Nothing!* And now you have the gross insensitivity to turn up here asking for a *piece of jewellery. Do you have no compassion? Do you have no sense of human decency?*' Visibly shaken by her own outburst, she took several deep breaths and he found himself staring at her mouth, captivated by the soft, ripe curve of her lower lip. The slight fullness gave an impression of sensuality while a tiny dimple in the corner of her mouth hinted at vulnerability.

The atmosphere throbbed with tension and Nikos forced himself to remember that Angie Littlewood was a woman to whom sensuality was entirely foreign. 'The very first words I spoke to you were of condolence.'

She was standing right in front of him now, chin lifted, eyes blazing into his. A faint scent teased his nostrils and he wondered for a moment whether she was woman enough to enjoy perfume and then decided that what he could smell was probably her shampoo.

'Words are nothing without the appropriate feeling behind them and we both know that you are entirely devoid of feeling.' She spat the words angrily and he ground his teeth.

'I make excuses for your behaviour because I know you are distressed about your sister.'

She gasped. '*My* behaviour? I'm not the one who seduced and misled an innocent young girl—who made her so utterly miserable she drank herself into oblivion and then fell to her death. I think if we're examining anyone's behaviour here it should be yours but the difference is that I'm not prepared to excuse you. You are a ruthless, self-seeking, egocentric *bastard*—' She stopped as she said the word and lifted a hand to her mouth, shock and confusion on her pale face. 'I—I'm sorry,' she began stiffly and he raised an eyebrow, wondering why she felt the need to apologise.

'Sorry for what? For using the same language that your sister frequently used?'

Colour touched her cheeks. 'We're not—I mean, I'm not—' She gave a faint frown as if she were trying to remember the point of their argument. 'You think of nothing but money and possessions and you need to be taught that there are other things that matter. I'm not prepared to give you your jewel.' Her voice cracked. 'It was the last thing she was wearing. I can't—why would you need it, anyway? It was supposed to be given to the woman of your heart and we both know that you don't have a heart, Mr Kyriacou.'

Not prepared to give him the diamond?

Nikos stared at her in a state of stunned disbelief. It hadn't occurred to him, even for a moment, that she'd seriously refuse to hand over the jewel.

Shaken by the less than welcome knowledge that he'd underestimated an opponent for the first time in his life, Nikos stood frozen to the spot, watching as she strode from the room and slammed the door so hard that the sound echoed round the abandoned lecture theatre for several seconds.

Nikos stared after her, his brain still filled with the vision of flashing blue eyes and fiery red hair.

What, he thought to himself, was he going to do now?

CHAPTER THREE

WHAT on earth had her sister ever seen in the man?

Still shocked and shaking from the unexpected violence of her own temper, Angie twisted her hair on top of her head and secured it with a vicious stab of the clip.

If she was honest, she was more than a little horrified by the strength of her own reaction. If she'd been asked to describe her character in two words she would have chosen 'calm' and 'logical'. But where had logic been today when she'd stood in front of Nikos Kyriacou and called him a bastard? And as for calm—

She cringed at the memory. She'd raised her voice and used language that she considered to be extremely distasteful. *She'd sounded more like her mother than herself.* But maybe her mother was right, in this instance. Nikos Kyriacou had behaved badly. It didn't matter which way you looked at it, the evidence was there. He'd dated her sister—the gift of the necklace supported her sister's claim that he'd been in love with her and intending to marry her, so there could be little doubt that she was telling the truth on that score—and then the relationship had ended. And the Greek's sole purpose in life was now to retrieve the necklace he'd given away so carelessly. Ready for the next woman, no doubt.

Angie gritted her teeth. She was the first to admit that relationships weren't exactly her forte, but it was obvious to her that Nikos Kyriacou had never intended to marry her sister and his track record supported that assumption. According to her mother, he never dated a woman for longer than three weeks. Clearly her sister had been severely misled.

Angie pushed her files into her bag and then lifted a hand to her chest just to reassure herself that the diamond was still there, safely tucked under her jumper.

Perhaps it had been foolish to wear it, but wearing it had made her feel closer to Tiffany and it wasn't as if anyone could see it. Under her jumper was probably as safe a place as any until she gave it back to the Kyriacou family.

She should have done it today, of course. She should have reached inside her boring roll-neck jumper, undone the clasp and given him the diamond. And that would have been the end of it, at least for him. But for her—

She just couldn't bear to part with something that Tiffany had worn.

Which was ridiculous, she thought miserably as she pushed open the door and walked up the stairs that led to the exit, because she could hardly go through life wearing high neck jumpers to conceal a priceless diamond. She was going to have to stop being so sentimental and give it back. It didn't matter that touching a jewel that Tiffany had worn somehow brought comfort. She was going to have to find her comfort in other ways.

It was time to do the right thing.

Time to return the jewel.

'Are you all right? I wanted to check on you.' Helen Knightly hovered in the doorway and Angie looked up from her computer and adjusted her glasses.

Two days had passed and she'd heard nothing from Nikos Kyriacou but, oddly enough, his silence was more disturbing than his presence. She didn't trust him. 'I'm fine, thank you. Honestly.'

'I'm sorry about the other day.' Her boss was clutching a newspaper. 'When he arrived in my office demanding to see you, I tried to suggest that he make an appointment but he didn't take no for an answer.'

Angie gave a wan smile. 'No. He doesn't appear to be very good at hearing that word.'

'I suppose it was nice that he wanted to come and apologise in person.'

Under the cover of her desk, Angie's toes curled in her shoes. 'Absolutely.' She had no intention of revealing that the purpose of Nikos Kyriacou's visit had had little to do with contrition and everything to do with greed.

'It must have been hard for him too, losing a girlfriend.' Helen Knightly sighed and held out the newspaper she was holding. 'I think you ought to see this before anyone else shows you. It's a little upsetting, I suppose, but you have to remember that he's obviously trying to get on with his life just as you are, which has to be a good thing. How's your mother?'

'She's fine,' Angie said absently, taking the paper with a flicker of disquiet. *A little upsetting?* What exactly would be in a newspaper that she would find upsetting? 'What do you mean, "he's obviously trying to get on with his life"?'

'Page two story: "*Greek tycoon seeks consolation after villa tragedy.*"'

Her mouth dry and her heart pounding, Angie opened the paper with shaking hands and found herself faced with a large picture of Nikos Kyriacou emerging from a nightclub in close contact with a tall willowy blonde.

Angie stared down at the paper, a dangerous cocktail of

emotions mingling inside her. Shock, pain and anger tangled together and she dropped the paper on to the desk and sucked in a deep breath to try and calm herself.

Was that why he was so desperate to repossess the jewel? So that he could give it to another woman?

Helen made an apologetic sound. 'Perhaps I shouldn't have shown you—'

'You were right to show me.' As if in a trance, Angie stood up, trying to clear her thoughts and control herself. Feeling slightly dazed, she looked at Helen, her expression bewildered. 'Have you ever thought you knew yourself really well, only to discover that you're not the person you thought you were?'

Helen's expression was puzzled. 'Well, no, I don't suppose I have, but you've suffered a severe shock, my dear, had a terrible loss to cope with. It's natural that you should be feeling strange and a little unsettled, if that's what's worrying you.'

'I don't feel strange or unsettled.' She felt—*furious*. Bitterly angry that Nikos Kyriacou could be allowed to brush off the matter of her sister's death as nothing more than a minor inconvenience. Absolutely boiling mad that he would happily date another woman in full view of the press without so much as a flicker of conscience or the slightest concession to decency. Had he given any thought at all to what such a picture would do to her already grieving mother?

The desire to seriously hurt him grew and grew inside her and she curled her fists into her palms and understood for the first time in her life what it was like to want revenge. For the first time she had some understanding of what had driven her mother to urge her to seek justice. She was so blisteringly angry with him, so insulted and hurt by his careless, arrogant behaviour that she wanted to make him suffer.

She sank down on to the chair, still holding the newspaper as she tried to calm herself down. *Tried to remember who she was.* She was a respected archaeologist. She was an educated woman—a pacifist who believed totally in the use of negotiation as a means of solving disputes. She didn't believe in 'an eye for an eye and a tooth for a tooth'. She didn't believe in vengeance.

So why did she suddenly want to find a way of hurting Nikos Kyriacou the way he'd hurt her sister?

'Go home.' Helen stepped forward and prised the newspaper from her numb fingers. 'Really, I think you need a few days off. You can't expect to get over this in a hurry and I'm sure that seeing Mr Kyriacou has made everything seem very raw.'

'Yes. Yes, it has.' Still slightly dazed by the onslaught of emotions that battered her brain, Angie switched off her computer and rose to her feet with a distracted nod of her head. 'I need some fresh air. I don't feel like me any more. But I want to keep that newspaper. Can I have it, please?'

Reluctantly Helen handed it to her and urged her towards the door. 'Go and see the doctor. Take a sedative or something. Don't come back until you're ready.'

Hardly aware of what she was doing, Angie pushed the newspaper into her bag and walked up the stone steps. She elbowed her way through crowds of the public admiring the dinosaur exhibition at the front of the museum and pushed through the revolving doors into the street.

Oblivious to the curious glances of passers-by, she walked in a state of blind misery, her thoughts on her sister. Tiffany had been so young and naïve. Being given the necklace must have meant so much to her. Whereas to him it had meant nothing at all

Without even realising what she was doing, Angie lifted a hand to the jewel that was safely hidden under her roll-neck top. Wearing it gave her a comfort that she couldn't explain, even to herself. Just knowing that she was wearing something that Tiffany had worn made her feel better.

It started to rain, but Angie didn't notice. How had Tiffany felt when she'd realised that Nikos Kyriacou had no intention of marrying her? How had she felt when she'd discovered that the relationship had meant nothing? Had Nikos Kyriacou been seeing other women when he was with her sister?

Tears started to fall but her face was so wet from the rain that no one even noticed. They were too busy trying to escape from the weather to notice her distress.

She walked home on automatic pilot and slotted her key into the front door with a shaking hand.

The first thing she saw as she walked into the house was a half full glass of whisky on the kitchen table. Scraping her soaking wet hair away from her face, she lifted the offending glass and stared at it in despair. Her mother had been drinking *again*. She was going to pour it away, along with all the alcohol in the house.

The doorbell rang and Angie glanced towards the sink and then gave an impatient sigh and turned towards the front door instead, the glass still in her hand. It would be the neighbours, checking on her mother and she didn't want them to worry.

Wondering how her life had deteriorated to this level, she yanked open the front door.

Nikos Kyriacou stood on the doorstep, an expression of simmering impatience on his cold, handsome face. 'I will come straight to the point. I have tried to tackle this subject with as much tact and sensitivity as I am able but you refuse to meet me even halfway so the time has come to stop playing games.' His gaze fastened on the glass in her hand and the impatience in his eyes changed to incredulity. 'Clearly the use of alcohol as a crutch runs in the family.'

Standing in the doorway holding a glass of whisky wasn't

exactly the impression of herself that she would have chosen to give another person, but his judgemental tone and the look of contempt in his eyes squashed any feelings of embarrassment that she might otherwise have suffered. The tension and pressure had been building all day and something inside her suddenly snapped. 'Tact and sensitivity? When did you ever show tact and sensitivity? Certainly not in my hearing. Given that you are the cause of *all* our current problems, I advise you to leave now while your limbs are still attached to your body.'

Thick, dark lashes lowered, shielding the expression in his eyes. 'By all means blame me if it makes you feel better,' he drawled in a soft tone, 'but we both know that I can hardly be held responsible for your sister's drink problem.'

'No?' Her misery and grief turned to furious anger. 'My sister had the misfortune to spend time with *you*, Mr Kyriacou. That in itself is surely sufficient justification for alcoholic support. Having met you and spent time with you, I can understand all too easily why she would have found herself in need of that support.' Her tone was acid. 'I should imagine it was the only way my poor sister could get through the day. If I were in the unfortunate position of being forced into your company on a regular basis, I too would drink to excess, I can assure you.'

His eyes moved slowly over her hair and face and she was suddenly uncomfortably aware of the contrast between her soaking wet, ultra ordinary appearance and the svelte, perfectly groomed woman she'd seen him with in the newspaper.

His smile was faintly contemptuous as if the mere thought of her being in his company was laughable. 'There is no way you would ever find yourself spending time with me on a regular basis. You are not the sort of woman I would ever willingly seek out.' The bored derision in his tone was deliberately insulting and she gave a soft gasp of outrage.

'I think you'd better go.' She started to close the door, but Nikos Kyriacou planted a foot inside the hallway and shouldered his way through.

'I've already told you, I'm tired of playing games.' He pushed the door shut with the palm of his hand, his expression grim as he stared at her. 'Once you have returned my property, I will leave.'

'Your broke my sister's heart. You promised to marry her.'

His voice cool and unemotional, Nikos took a step backwards. 'I *never* would have married someone like your sister. It is laughable to think I would have considered it.'

Angie gasped, both at the words and his derisive tone. 'You just don't care, do you? Her death means nothing to you but a logistical inconvenience. You'd better leave. Now.'

'Removing myself from the company of your appalling family is my highest priority. Unfortunately I cannot leave until the necklace is restored to *my* family.' Clearly he thought he was slumming it by having to deal with them and his blatant distaste goaded her still further. It didn't matter that she, herself, had been shocked and embarrassed by both her sister and mother's behaviour in the past. All that mattered now was the fact that he had judged Tiffany good enough to sleep with but not to marry.

'The necklace no longer belongs to you. A gift is a gift. Maybe you'll remember that next time you give away something valuable.'

Nikos didn't flinch. 'The necklace did *not* belong to your sister.'

'Well, she was wearing it when she died,' Angie reminded him helpfully, 'so, unless you're suggesting that she stole it, then it appears to now be in our possession. Perhaps the loss of the necklace will force you to rethink your lifestyle, Mr Kyriacou. You say that you would never have married a girl like my sister, but you were more than happy to seduce her, were you not? You came here, so soon after her death, not to sympathise or offer condolences but to demand the return of a gift. What sort of cold, unfeeling monster does that make you, I wonder?'

His explosion of temper was as sudden as it was shocking as he turned on her with a dangerous flash of his eyes and let out a stream of fluent Greek that contained words that she hadn't encountered before. But, even if her knowledge of the Greek language hadn't allowed her to pick up the gist of his diatribe, the threatening expression on his bronzed handsome face was more than sufficient to provide adequate translation.

The volcanic force of his anger made her want to seek refuge under the nearest table and she had to force herself to keep her own expression impassive, determined not to reveal either that he'd frightened her or that she spoke his language.

'Shouting isn't going to change the facts. Nor is ranting in a foreign language.'

He took a deep breath and stabbed bronzed fingers through his glossy dark hair. 'Despite what you may believe, I sincerely regret your sister's death and a full investigation was conducted by the appropriate authorities, as I've already told you.' His English was heavily accented, as if the sudden switch of language had thrown him. 'The truth is that, had your sister drunk less, she wouldn't now be dead.'

Angie's expression was stony as she fixed her eyes on his. 'The truth is that had you not given her a *reason* to drink she wouldn't now be dead. You need to be more responsible in your relationships, Mr Kyriacou.'

The air hissed through his teeth. 'I'm *extremely* responsible in my relationships.'

'Really?' Angie picked up her bag and dragged out the newspaper. 'Who's she, then? Some convenient bimbo you picked up last night? Or do you need the necklace so that you can give it to her as proof of your undying love and devotion?'

He stared at the picture in the paper and a muscle worked in his lean cheek. 'She's no one important.'

'No one important? Does she know that?'

'The press photograph me all the time. It's an obsession.'

'How very inconvenient for you.' *All he cared about was his image.* 'It must be almost impossible to conduct your affairs in private. I really couldn't care less who you sleep with, Mr Kyriacou, except to feel the most sincere sympathy for them. My point is merely that this photograph shows you to be decidedly lacking in sensitivity genes. Six months ago my sister was wearing your necklace around her throat and partying in your villa. Now we're mourning her death and you are out seeking a replacement. The facts are right in front of me, so don't try and tell me that you care and have feelings.'

'I don't plan to tell you anything. I'm not in the habit of explaining myself to anyone.'

'Well, you should be! Being rich and bossy doesn't give you the right to walk all over people.'

He looked at her then, his gaze disturbingly intense as it rested on her face. 'You really do have a most unfortunate personality.' His voice was silky-smooth and the stillness of his powerful frame was possibly more intimidating than his volcanic burst of temper. 'Perhaps if you spent less time examining bones and pieces of pottery and more time on personal relationships, your mood might improve. Even if it were possible to overlook your complete lack of interest in your appearance, take it from me, if there's one thing guaranteed to turn a guy off it's hysteria. You might want to work on that.'

It was the final straw. The suggestion that she even *cared* what he thought about her should have made her laugh but instead misery bubbled inside her. He was so superficial. He had no conscience and nothing she said seemed to make him see that he'd behaved abominably.

'You can't have your necklace back.' She blurted the words out in a rush. 'To you it's just currency. A way of buying sex, but to me—'

'Yes, Dr Littlewood?' His tone was silky-smooth. 'To you it's what?'

How could she possibly tell him the truth? *That having the necklace round her neck was comforting. It made her feel closer to Tiffany.* She realised how completely ridiculous that would sound to a man like him. A man who didn't have a gentle or compassionate bone in his body. 'I just—I just want it.'

'Of course you do. It's the passport to a lifestyle beyond your wildest dreams.'

All he thought about was money.

Distraught about her sister and deeply offended by his insensitivity, she flung the contents of the glass in his face but even his soft curse and the blatant shock on his handsome features weren't sufficient to satisfy her. She wanted to hurt him. She really, *really* wanted to hurt him. If she'd held a gun at that moment she would have shot him through the heart without caring for the consequences.

As it was, she was going to have to settle for something less than a mortal wound.

Revenge.

Wasn't that what her mother had said? Hadn't she said that revenge was the only language that a Greek male like Nikos Kyriacou would understand? Well, maybe she was right.

'You want your jewel?' She watched him wipe the beads of liquid from his face with his strong fingers, saw the simmering fury build in his dark eyes. Willing to bet that it wasn't often that anyone won a round with Nikos Kyriacou, she savoured the moment. 'You can have it. But there's a condition.'

Without further comment, he reached inside his jacket and removed a cheque book. 'Name your price. Whatever it is will be worth it to remove your entire family from my life.'

'Ah, but you see, that isn't what's going to happen,' Angie said, her voice shaking. 'Money would be too easy for you. You wouldn't even feel it and I want you to feel it. I really, *really* want you to feel it. In return for the jewel, you are going to give me the one thing you always refused to give my sister.'

He was ominously still. 'I don't understand you.'

'You're going to marry me.' Her heart was pounding against her chest. She still couldn't quite believe what she'd said. 'You wouldn't marry my sister, but you're going to have to marry me if you want that jewel back, Nikos.' Her flippant use of his first name was blatantly insulting and there was a long throbbing silence as he studied her with barely contained aggression.

Who was more shocked? she wondered. Her or him?

When he finally spoke, his voice was hoarse. '*Meu Dios,* you *have* to be joking.' His Greek accent was suddenly pronounced. 'I would never marry a woman like you.'

She wasn't hurt by that comment, she told herself firmly. In fact it was good that he clearly found her repellent. The more repulsive she appeared to him, the greater the punishment. 'It's a real test of character, don't you think? Just how far are you prepared to go for this one jewel? Are you prepared to marry a woman with an unfortunate personality who takes no pride in her appearance?'

He stood in rigid silence, his eyes stormy, his mouth set in a hard line.

Definitely he was Ares, she thought to herself with a flicker of trepidation. *The Greek god of war.* Handsome, but vain and cruel. Priorities in all the wrong places.

'Why would you even suggest this? Why would a woman

like you—' his dark eyes swept over her in a disparaging look
'—possibly want to marry me?'

'I don't want to marry you.' Angie kept her voice calm.
'I'm sure that comes as a surprise to you, given your natural
arrogance, but it's the truth. I have absolutely no wish to
marry you. In fact, since we're going for honesty here, I
probably ought to confess that I find the prospect of spending
time with you extremely distasteful.' She saw him straighten
his shoulders. Saw the disbelief in his eyes.

'Women are queuing up to spend time with me.'

'Well, you're very rich,' Angie muttered, 'and that has to
be advantageous for someone so mercenary and totally
lacking in interpersonal skills.' Something flashed in his eyes
and for a brief terrifying moment she wondered whether she'd
gone too far. Then the breath hissed through his teeth.

'If that is truly your opinion of me, then why would you
make such a ridiculous suggestion?'

'Marriage, you mean? Because to force you to marry me
would be the sweetest revenge.' Wondering what on earth
had come over her, she ploughed on. 'You can't stand me, can
you? It pains you to even be near me. You can't wait to remove
me from your life. Well, it isn't going to happen. You gave my
sister a two-year contract with your company, so let's switch
the agreement. Two years, Nikos. You have to agree to stay
married to me for two years.'

His jaw was clenched tight and she knew he was struggling
not to release a stream of invective. 'You too would be in this
marriage that you propose.'

'But the fundamental difference between us is that I have
absolutely no interest in marrying anyone else so I might as
well marry you. It would be entertaining, I think, to cramp
your style and watch you squirm.'

He stared at her with incredulity. 'You ask for the impossible.'

'Nothing is impossible if you want it badly enough. Just how badly do you want your precious jewel, Nikos?'

He studied her for a long intense moment. 'I have extremely powerful reasons for wanting that jewel.'

'I'm sure you do. And all of them are financial.'

A muscle twitched in his cheek. 'You don't understand anything about the situation, but if marrying you is the only way that the jewel can be returned to me, then I agree to your terms. Fortunately for you I'm feeling generous, so I'll give you twenty-four hours to rethink your offer. I advise you to think hard.'

'Offer?' Dizzy with shock that he'd accepted her suggestion, she gave a humourless laugh, squashing down the sudden impulse to run and hide. 'It wasn't an offer, Mr Kyriacou, it was a threat.'

'Yes.' His smile was dangerous. 'But a threat to whom, *agape mou*? Ask yourself that while you are lying there congratulating yourself on victory. Twenty-four hours. I'll see you tomorrow.'

Why did she suddenly have the feeling that he was the one in control?

His assumption that she'd be sitting around waiting for him outraged her. 'I'm not in tomorrow. Actually, I have a date,' she said on impulse and then winced, reluctant to examine the motives that had driven her to refer to her colleague as a 'date'. 'I'm going to a lecture on the protogeometric art of Crete at the museum with a special friend.'

He studied her for a moment and a faintly derisive smile touched his hard mouth. 'You really know how to let your hair down, don't you, Dr Littlewood? You're a regular party animal. I'll see you tomorrow.'

Without giving her the opportunity to argue, he turned and strode out of the house, slamming the door behind him and leaving her boiling with frustration.

* * *

The restaurant was cheap, the meat tough and badly cooked and Angie prodded the food on her plate, trying to show interest in Cyril's earnest summary of the lecture they'd just attended.

Why was she finding it so hard to concentrate? And why, all of a sudden, was she noticing things about him that she'd never noticed before? *Things that she'd never considered to be important.* Like the fact that his hair was slightly too long and untidy, his beard decidedly goaty and his checked shirt a painful clash with the ancient herringbone jacket that was probably a throwback to his university days. And, as for the way he ate—

She looked away from his open mouth, slightly revolted that his desire to talk appeared to be in no way impeded by his appetite. Suddenly she found herself comparing Cyril's complete lack of social grace with Nikos Kyriacou's smooth sophistication. An image of glossy dark hair and an arrogant stare filled her brain and she caught herself with a faint frown of annoyance. Why was she wasting a single thought on the man? Appearance didn't matter to her. She didn't judge people on such shallow terms. All right, so she couldn't imagine Nikos Kyriacou eating with his mouth open and he certainly was astonishingly handsome but he was also a nasty person.

Possibly aware that he was losing her attention, Cyril leaned towards her as he talked, spraying food over the tablecloth, stabbing with a fork to illustrate the point he was making, and she shrank away slightly, reminding herself that he had an amazing intellect. It was only when Cyril stuttered to a halt in mid sentence and stared in astonishment at a point behind her left shoulder that she turned and saw Nikos Kyriacou standing by their table.

In a restaurant full of students and academic types watching their budget, he looked entirely out of place in his immaculate dark suit and silk shirt. Like a dish of caviare placed among plates of mass produced frozen pizza, she reflected absently, or a bottle of vintage champagne lined up alongside jugs of pond water. Just in a completely different class. Not that he was paying any attention to those around him. The focus of that hard, cold stare was *her.*

She shifted slightly under his unflinching scrutiny, aware that they were suddenly the subject of intense speculation by other diners.

'What are you doing here?'

'Twenty-four hours are up,' he reminded her in silky tones, enviably indifferent to the interest of those around him. On the tables closest to them, people had actually stopped eating, obviously aware that this was something worth watching.

'I'm on a date.'

His gaze flickered to Cyril and there was sympathy and amusement in his eyes. 'You find her company pleasurable?'

Cyril's cheeks turned a mottled puce colour. 'Dr Littlewood has the keenest brain I've ever encountered,' he stuttered, dropping his fork and paper napkin simultaneously. 'Her research into the methods used by—'

'I'm sure her conversation can be very stimulating,' Nikos drawled in a bored tone, silencing him with a lift of his bronzed hand, 'although, speaking personally, the ability to converse about ancient pots isn't at the top of the list of qualities I demand in a woman. In fact, when I'm on a "date" I don't care if we don't talk at all.'

The implication of his words wasn't lost on Cyril and the mottled puce colour deepened and spread into his hair.

Completely mortified, Angie half rose to her feet. 'Fortunately not everyone is like you.' She kept her voice low, determined not to be overheard by the people at the next table. 'You're disgusting, do you know that?'

His features were impassive. 'That's no way to speak to your husband, *agape mou*. You need to learn some respect.'

She stilled. 'You're not my—'

'No, I'm not.' A faint smile touched his hard mouth. 'But I will be.'

Her heart stumbled. 'I didn't think—'

'No—' The smile widened. 'You *definitely* didn't think and it's entirely possible that you'll come to regret that fact very shortly. But it's too late for regret, because I've decided to accept your offer. The answer is yes, I will marry you.'

Cyril gave a strangled gasp and knocked his glass over. Cheap red wine poured over the tablecloth and dripped slowly on to the floor. 'Angie? You asked *this man* to marry you?'

'Very enlightened, don't you think?' His tone casual, Nikos reached out and closed strong fingers round Angie's wrist, jerking her to her feet. 'Some men might be put off by such brazen behaviour but I get very turned on by a woman who knows her own mind. In my experience they're usually complete animals in bed.'

Deeply humiliated by his words and the fact that he hadn't made the slightest effort to lower his voice, Angie tugged at her wrist, aware that Cyril was gaping at her along with just about every other person in the restaurant. 'Let me go.'

Nikos tightened his grip and tugged her against him. 'To have and to hold,' he reminded her in smooth tones. 'At the moment I'm doing the holding bit, but later on we'll get to the "having" part of the arrangement and I predict that it will be *extremely* interesting.'

Unbelievably shocked and wishing she could just melt through the floor, Angie yanked at her wrist but failed to free herself. She couldn't remember a moment in her life when she'd felt so completely humiliated. 'I think we should continue this conversation outside.'

'I entirely agree. I've never really been into the whole group thing.' Nikos summoned a waiter with an imperious lift of his free hand. 'And, speaking of which, you ought to know that I don't actually allow my future wife to dine with another man, so if you want to say goodbye then do it now while I settle the bill. But no physical contact, please, especially no kissing.' He handed a card to the waiter and Angie took a step backwards, feeling physically sick at the thought of actually kissing Cyril.

'It's typical of you to reduce everything to the physical. My relationship with Cyril is on a much higher level than anything you can possibly understand,' she said tightly and Nikos gave a careless shrug of his broad shoulders.

'I don't really care what level my relationships are on providing they're conducted in the horizontal plane.'

Angie enjoyed a brief but satisfying mental image of Cyril standing up and thumping Nikos hard but in reality he sat frozen in his chair, a look of stupefied disbelief on his face. And anyway, she thought gloomily, there was no doubting who the winner would be in any physical encounter. A man like Cyril, with his slightly bony hairless wrists sticking out from beyond a jacket that was much too small for him, was absolutely no match for Nikos, who was a prime specimen of athletic, muscled Greek manhood.

She gave a frown and a slight shake of her head, horrified by the direction of her thoughts. Cyril was a respected academic. A civilised person. He wouldn't ever stoop so low as to indulge in physical confrontation and she wouldn't want him to. She didn't approve of such behaviour. On the other hand, she would have at least expected him to use some of his intellectual skills to deliver an appropriate verbal put-down.

She turned to him, frustrated that he would allow himself to be treated so badly. 'Cyril—say something.'

'Yes, please do feel free to contribute to the discussion.' Nikos raised an eyebrow in mocking anticipation and Cyril spluttered slightly and half rose to his feet.

'I—I can afford to pay for our meal.'

Angie ground her teeth and Nikos gave a half smile, clearly all too aware of her frustration. 'I'm sure you can in a place like this. Consider it compensation,' he drawled in a bored tone as he settled the bill and pocketed his card. His eyes rested on Angie for a long moment, his gaze faintly mocking. 'Although, on reflection, you should probably be the one paying me to take her away. I'm doing you a favour. She would have made you miserable.'

'And you think she can m-make you happy?' Stammering and virtually incoherent with shock and surprise, Cyril rose to his feet but Nikos gently pushed him back into his seat.

'She's going to make me extremely *unhappy*,' he said softly, 'which I believe was her intention when she proposed. But nowhere near as unhappy as I intend to make her. And at least I know I won't be bored.'

Without giving the shell-shocked Cyril time to compose a suitable response, Nikos strode from the restaurant, virtually dragging Angie after him. He pushed his way through the door of the restaurant and out on to the pavement without breaking stride and virtually threw her into the back of the black limousine waiting on the kerb.

CHAPTER FOUR

SPRAWLED inelegantly over the sumptuous leather seat, Angie tried to right herself. Her hair had tumbled from the knot at the back of her head and her cheeks were flushed. Her loss of dignity disturbed her and she rounded on him in anger. 'How *dare* you create such a scene in a public place? And you were *unforgivably* rude to Cyril. You've just left him sitting there!'

Nikos leaned forward and issued a string of instructions in rapid Greek. Instantly the driver manoeuvred the car into the traffic.

'If he cared that much then he shouldn't have let me take you away.' He settled himself back in the seat. 'And you were just dying for him to stop me, weren't you? Just longing for him to stand up and thump me.'

The fact that he'd been able to read her so well was extremely frustrating. 'Cyril would never do anything so grossly uncivilised.'

'No, he probably wouldn't, but try not to be upset about it.' His tone sympathetic, he stretched his long legs out in front of him, the expression on his handsome face unbearably smug. 'You're with a real man now.'

She stared at his cold, handsome face in disbelief. 'You're

insufferably arrogant. I don't know how any woman can stand you.'

'Well, if Cyril is an example of your taste in men then I can understand your confusion.' His voice was a languorous drawl, his eyes lingering on her face in mocking contemplation. 'But the truth, *agape mou*, is that you find me almost unbearably exciting, don't you? You can't stop making comparisons and you just *hate* that because you like to think that you're above having such a basic human need as a desire for sex, but secretly you're absolutely longing for it.'

She gasped. 'I don't find you exciting.'

'You do. It's just that you don't recognise the feeling because up until now your life has been totally devoid of the feeling and I'm sure that's entirely natural if you've been mixing with men like Cyril.'

'I repeat,' she said with a soft gasp, 'I *don't* find you exciting. And I'm *certainly* not longing for sex. Why do you have to reduce everything to its most basic? If you must know, I happen to be more interested in the human mind than the human body.' She knew her cheeks were pink but couldn't help it. She'd never had a conversation like this before in her life. Sex wasn't something she talked about.

'The human race is basic. If it wasn't then we wouldn't survive.' Thick, dark lashes lowered slightly as he studied her. 'Man was born with an urge to procreate. It's an entirely inbred and natural urge.'

She felt the slow spread of warmth between her thighs and her hands clenched into fists on her lap. 'I suppose that's your justification for your irresponsible sex life.'

'Active sex life,' he corrected her gently. 'Active.'

The term conjured up more images that she didn't want to face. Nikos, his hard athletic body entwined with that of some pathetically willing woman. 'So you're just doing your bit for mankind?' She used sarcasm to hide the growing tumble of emotions inside her.

'I'm saying that hot sex between a man and a woman who are attracted to each other is entirely natural.'

Hot sex? The colour in her face deepened and she grew more and more uncomfortable. 'You're entitled to your opinion, of course, but some of us have different priorities in life. Personally, I find a mental connection more stimulating than anything that happens physically.'

He smiled, maddeningly relaxed and at ease. 'Our priorities are often set by our experiences. You're more interested in the mind because you've spent your entire life in the company of men like Cyril who have nothing else to offer.'

Her heart was pounding hard against her chest. 'Cyril is more stimulating company than you will ever be.'

'Really?' Nikos leaned forward, his eyes never leaving her face. 'Does he make your heart race and your breath catch, Dr Littlewood? When you're with him is your body on fire? In bed together, does he make you forget you're an archaeologist? Does he make you forget absolutely everything except the fact that you're a woman?'

She stared at him, hypnotised, so shocked that it took her a moment to find her voice. Then the colour flooded into her cheeks and she looked away quickly, staring out of the window in an attempt to calm herself. 'It's typical of you to reduce everything to sex but my relationship with Cyril isn't like that.'

'I find it all too easy to believe you.' His tone bordered on the derogatory. 'You probably both approach sex like an academic exercise, consulting the appropriate texts in order to derive evidential support in favour of the physical act.'

She whipped her head round at that, just furious with him! 'I'm not interested in having sex with Cyril!'

'You shouldn't blame yourself for that,' he assured her in sympathetic tones. 'I'm sure most women would feel the same way. He isn't the right guy for you. You need someone more physical to break down all those barriers you've built up around yourself.'

She didn't even want to think about it! Her whole body was trembling and she felt hot inside and out of control in a way that she didn't understand. 'I've had enough of this. Stop the car and let me out. I insist that you stop the car. I don't want to spend another moment in your company.'

'You should have thought of that before you proposed,' he pointed out, his eyes suddenly hard. 'You're the one who wanted to be my wife and that position comes with certain rules, I'm afraid. One of them is that no wife of mine is permitted to be with another man. Even someone with such a dubious claim on masculinity as your Cyril.'

'He's not *my* Cyril.' She struggled to wriggle her foot back into the shoe that had somehow become parted from her foot during her less than elegant entrance into the car. She felt flustered and completely out of her comfort zone. She'd never had a conversation like this with anyone before and she found it hideously uncomfortable.

'No, you're right, he isn't your Cyril.' His smile was less than pleasant. 'At least, not any more.'

She jammed her foot hard into her shoe and brushed the hair out of her eyes. 'You have absolutely no right to tell me who I can and can't see.'

'I'm Greek,' he reminded her gently, the hard glint in his eyes negating the apology in his tone. 'We're a very possessive race, I'm afraid. Not that great at sharing. Sorry, but that's just the way it is. I'm sure you'll learn to live with it. You probably ought to be grateful to me. You never would have been happy with a man like him.'

'You're doing this on purpose! You're trying to make me loathe you *so much* that I just give you the jewel to get you out of my life. Well, it isn't going to happen. You are not going to get away with treating women badly any longer. This time, you're going to pay the price.'

The driver steered the car through the heavy London traffic and Angie sat back against the seat, fuming. *And panicking.* She realised suddenly that she hadn't actually believed for a moment that he'd agree to her proposition and the implications of her revenge plan suddenly hit home. She was used to a quiet, ordered life. Never would she have described herself as a tense person but every time Nikos strolled into the room her stress levels seemed to rocket. Her insides churned and her whole body behaved in a way that was completely inexplicable. It was all very well forcing him to marry her, but how was she going to stand being with him day after day? He'd be in the office, she reminded herself quickly. And she could always find somewhere quiet to read in the evenings.

And anyway, none of this was about her. It was about Tiffany. She owed it to her sister to at least make him *think* about what he'd done.

But what about him? Why had a man like him, a man who had spent his entire adult life avoiding commitment, accepted the idea of marriage so readily?

Did he want the jewel that badly or was marriage to her simply not as distasteful as she'd believed it would be?

She looked at him for a moment, studying his cold, handsome face through narrowed eyes and suddenly knew exactly why the idea of marriage didn't disturb him as much as it should. Obviously he wasn't the sort of man to allow a little thing like a wedding to stand in the way of his continual pursuit of women. Just like her father, he was clearly planning to have numerous extramarital affairs and if he did that then it would defeat the purpose of forcing him to marry her. He wouldn't suffer at all.

What could she do? What could she do that would actually have an impact on him? Her mind working fast, she thought hard about the sort of man he was—*all the things she'd ever read about him.* Nikos was a prime example of man at its most basic. All that seemed to matter to him was sex. Inspiration struck and suddenly she knew *exactly* how she could make her revenge all the more sweet.

'I wish to see a lawyer,' she blurted out quickly. 'If we're going to get married then there are going to be certain conditions. I want a pre-nuptial agreement.'

He threw back his head and laughed in genuine amusement. 'If you think I would marry you *without* a pre-nuptial agreement then you truly know nothing about the man you're taking on. I've already told you, if you're hoping for money you can forget it because you won't get a single penny out of me. And why *you* would think you need a pre-nuptial agreement completely escapes me.'

She gave him a superior smile. 'That's because you don't tend to use your brain very much, do you? Like most men, you think with an entirely different part of your anatomy.'

She'd never imagined that such a powerfully built man could move so fast. He was as swift and silent as a predator closing in on its prey. One moment he was lounging with careless indifference against the furthest edge of the car, the next his hand was clamped in her hair and her body was pressed up against his as he held her captive. It was primal, basic, *male on female* and she felt everything inside her lurch.

'What are you doing?' Breathless, her heart pounding against her chest, she pushed at the hard muscle of his shoulders but he didn't shift. 'Get off! Let me go.'

'Do you know what I really think, *agape mou*?' His mouth

was so close to hers that she could feel his breath warming her lips and she didn't dare move even a fraction because then their mouths would touch. This close she could see the thickness of his lashes, the seductive curve of his mouth and the darkening shadow on his jaw. 'I think that after a less than stimulating evening staring at your Cyril, you're dying to know what it's like to be kissed by a man like me.'

She stared at him, hypnotised by the slumberous look in his molten eyes and the soft drawl of his slightly accented voice. 'I've told you a million times, he's isn't *my* Cyril and you have a ridiculously high opinion of yourself.'

'I have an entirely accurate opinion of myself,' he amended, 'whereas you don't appear to know yourself at all. I'm starting to think it might be interesting to show you who you really are. You, who spend your life unearthing the secrets of others, might be about to discover a few secrets about yourself.'

He felt hard, tough and masculine. Her stomach tumbled and lurched and she tried again to push him away. 'You're making me hot—'

'I know. I'm very experienced with women. I can tell that you're very turned on.' His voice was a soft purr and she felt her temper flare.

'I meant that the weather is too warm to have you lying on top of me.' She glared at him and he shifted away from her with athletic grace.

'Of course, if you want to blame the weather for your current hot flush then that's fine by me.'

She decided not to dignify his mocking statement with a reply. 'Where are we going?' Turned on? She wasn't turned on. She was outraged. She wriggled as far away from him as possible, aware of his gaze lingering on her hair. '*Stop* staring at me. And don't even *think* about telling me I need highlights and a haircut.'

He was silent for a moment, his eyes fixed on her hair. In fact he stared at her for so long that she started to squirm in her seat. All right, she knew that she probably didn't pay enough attention to her appearance, but did he really have to labour the point?

But before she could open her mouth and issue another verbal attack, he lifted a hand and touched her hair, twisting a silky strand round his long bronzed fingers. 'Your hair is a very unusual colour. Vibrant. Changing it would be nothing short of criminal.' His fingers slid slowly through her hair in a gesture that seemed astonishingly intimate. 'And I wouldn't say it needs cutting either. Most men find long hair more erotic in bed.'

Transfixed by the look in his eyes, she felt the temperature inside her soar to dangerous levels and jerked away from him. 'You're impossible! Do you really think I wear my hair long because it is more erotic in bed?'

'No.' He gave a slow smile and moved his hand, allowing her hair to fall back to her shoulder. 'I don't think you know the meaning of the word erotic.'

'Well, that's where you happen to be wrong,' she said primly, relieved to finally be on familiar ground. 'The word "erotic" derives from Eros, who was the God of love in Greek mythology and said by most legends to be the son of Aphrodite, the Goddess of love and Ares, the God of War.'

He studied her in silence for a moment and then gave a faint smile. 'Actually, many would argue with you on that point. Some believe that Eros was descended from Chaos and he was the God of Lust, not love. Of passion and sex.' His eyes were fixed on hers, his gaze disturbingly intense. 'But this is all very boring and I wasn't actually talking about the derivation of the word,' he said softly, his eyes sliding to her mouth. 'I was talking about the true meaning of the word in modern use, so let me now give you *my* definition.'

She shifted in her seat. 'I really don't—'

'Erotic is concerned with the most intense and arousing of sexual pleasure. When a woman uses her femininity as part of sexual stimulation, that's erotic. When a man gives in to powerful sexual desire and pleasures a woman, that's erotic. It's an orgy of sensual fulfilment, *agape mou*, not a word extracted from Greek mythology. To give it a more contemporary translation, erotic is carnal, erogenous, rousing, seductive, sexy, suggestive, voluptuous—'

'Stop it! Be quiet!' She put her hands over her ears, unable to listen to another word. For a moment she couldn't breathe at all and then his eyes lifted back to hers and suddenly she felt as though she had jumped straight into the deep end of a swimming pool from a great height. Out of her depth, she looked away from him, desperately trying to slow the rapid thump of her heart. His knowledge of Greek mythology surprised her but somehow he'd managed to take what could have been a stimulating academic discussion and lower it to the basest level. Which was entirely typical of him, she thought shakily. It was evident that, when he was with a woman, all he thought about was sex.

Consoling herself with the fact that she still held the trump card, she finally managed to steady her breathing and ignore the insidious throb deep in her body. 'I'm sure that the word "erotic" has featured frequently in your life in the past,' she said in a shaky voice, trying and failing to understand the burning ache between her thighs. 'Which is actually just as well because it certainly isn't going to feature in your life again in the future.'

'You think not?' Something about his deep velvety voice set her heart thumping again and she shifted in the seat.

'I *know* not.' Confused by her own feelings and furious with him for tying her in knots, she finally turned her head and looked at him. 'Aren't you going to ask me what I want written into the pre-nuptial agreement?'

'It's of very little interest to me.'

'Really?' Suddenly she wanted to do something to shake him out of his customary cool. She really, really wanted him to *mind* about something and as far as she could see, apart from money, there was only one thing that dominated his Neanderthal brain. 'I'm going to insist that the lawyer includes a clause which prevents you from having sexual relations with another woman. Once you marry me, you're going to live a celibate life, Nikos, so you'd better learn to say goodbye to all things erotic.'

A warm feeling of smug satisfaction spreading through her body, she settled back in her seat and waited for the reaction. But if she'd expected an explosion, then she was disappointed. Instead he lay sprawled in his seat, watching her from under half lowered lashes, the expression on his handsome face unreadable.

'You don't want me to have sex with another woman?' His gaze lingered on her face. 'You're absolutely sure about that?'

'Absolutely sure.' She smiled, confident that she was now back in control. 'And, if at any point during our marriage I'm shown evidence of your infidelity, then I won't reveal the whereabouts of the jewel.'

'You return the jewel to me on the day of our wedding, otherwise the deal doesn't go ahead.'

'If I did that, then you would simply divorce me.'

He gave a faint smile. 'I've instructed my lawyers to draw up an agreement which binds us together for two years, just as you requested. That should be more than enough for us to drive each other up the wall and for you to extract what you see as revenge. If you're in any doubt as to the depth of the punishment, then I can assure you that two years with you will be the equivalent of twenty years with any other woman.'

She absorbed the insult, telling herself that the more he loathed her, the more effective the revenge. 'So you agree to my terms?'

He suppressed a yawn. 'I agree not to have sex with other women for the duration of our marriage, if you're absolutely sure that's what you want. You might want to think hard before you confirm that point.'

She didn't need to think at all. She *knew* it was the right thing to do and was extremely glad she'd thought of it—and slightly surprised, if she were honest. Things pertaining to sex weren't usually high in her thoughts. She smiled, delighted that she'd won that point and wondering why he hadn't constructed a more vociferous argument in defence of his sex life. Or any argument, come to that. He'd been remarkably compliant considering the issue at stake. Surely a man as obsessed with sex as Nikos Kyriacou wouldn't so readily agree to having his activity in that area curbed for a full two years? *Wouldn't agree to celibacy?* On the other hand, he probably didn't want to reveal just how badly her punishment was affecting him. A man like him had an ego to protect. Except for the few occasions where she'd obviously driven him to the extreme limits of his patience, he clearly prided himself on his cool, unemotional approach to life. He was hardly going to display his true feelings on the matter.

Convinced that she had the upper hand for possibly the first time in days, Angie smiled at him, unable to hide her triumph. 'It's what I want.'

His eyes rested on her face and for a brief moment she thought she saw amusement in his gaze but then it was gone and he sat forward, hit a button that opened an intercom between him and the driver and issued another stream of instructions. 'We'll see the lawyer right away. Why wait?'

Her feeling of triumph faltered slightly in the face of his

indifference. Then she reminded herself that so far they'd spent less than an hour in each other's company. If he found her personality unfortunate on such relatively short acquaintance, she was surely guaranteed to cause him complete misery when they were joined in matrimony.

CHAPTER FIVE

Two weeks later, Angie sat waiting for the make-up artist to finish her work. 'Not too much. I don't usually wear make-up.' She couldn't quite believe that she'd allowed her mother to talk her into this. She would have been quite happy to just turn up at the wedding looking the way she always looked. It wasn't as if Nikos had any other expectations. He hadn't so much as mentioned a wedding dress or flowers. In fact, he'd treated their forthcoming nuptials in much the same vein as he might a business meeting.

She still smarted with indignation as she remembered his attitude during the visit to the lawyer. He'd virtually dragged her into the room and had then proceeded to ignore her, speaking entirely in Greek to the young, nervous lawyer seated behind the enormous desk. But even her fluency in his language hadn't helped her understand what was going on in his head. He'd instructed the man to ensure that the jewel became his on marriage.

Then they'd switched to English and it had been left to her to stumble out her wish that Nikos be banned from indulging in extramarital sex, a conversation she'd found painfully embarrassing to conduct with a third party.

Instead of looking annoyed, Nikos had lounged in a chair

in the furthest corner of the room, occasionally glancing at his watch as if he were being detained from something far more pressing than the simple matter of a pre-nuptial agreement.

In the car following their visit to the lawyer, he hadn't spoken to her. Instead he'd checked his emails on his Blackberry and made endless calls on his mobile phone, pausing only long enough to drop her home with the announcement that he'd send a car for her in two weeks' time. Then he'd driven off without a backward glance, leaving her seething and fuming.

It was clear that he wasn't allowing the prospect of marriage to interfere with his life in the slightest.

She frowned as the make-up artist stepped back and admired her work. Or maybe he was making the most of his last two weeks of freedom. Yes, that was probably it. Knowing him, Nikos was probably currently indulging in a sexual marathon of Olympian proportions. Something that would keep him going throughout his long sexless marriage to her.

Suddenly a disturbingly clear picture of Nikos's bronzed limbs entwined with creamy female flesh filled her brain and she blinked in shock, trying to dispel the image. What was it about him that made her think about sex when she wasn't even interested in sex?

She chewed at her freshly glossed lower lip, wondering what on earth she was letting herself in for. What had possessed her to demand all those things from him?

What had possessed her to insist on marriage when she wasn't in the least bit interested in marriage and even less so in marrying a man like Nikos, who had none of the qualities she admired in a person. He was probably quite clever, she conceded, or surely he wouldn't have been able to make such a success of his life but he clearly didn't require the slightest intellectual stimulation from his female companions. As long as they had blonde hair and were formed in the mould of Venus, he was happy.

Relieved that the make-up artist had finally finished, she stood up and examined her reflection in the mirror, failing to see a difference in herself. Even make up couldn't turn her into something she wasn't.

An image of the elegant blonde she'd seen him with in the paper taunted her and she took a step backwards, turning away from the mirror. Marrying her must indeed be the most hideous of punishments for a man like Nikos. All right, so she'd put away her glasses in favour of contact lenses and had allowed them to trim her hair and apply a little discreet make-up, but she still looked nothing like the women he usually escorted.

And that was a good thing, she told herself firmly. She was perfectly happy with the way she looked. She wasn't the slightest bit insecure. She *knew* she wasn't at all attractive in a physical sense and it really didn't bother her. It wasn't what mattered. She'd been given other, far more important gifts, like her brain. And the fact that Nikos didn't exactly regard intelligence as an asset was a good thing, wasn't it? She wanted him to suffer. That was the whole point of the exercise. He was going to be trapped with her. Committed to one woman for the first time in his life. It was surely justice at its most poetic.

'You look really worried,' the make-up artist said as she stood back to admire her handiwork. 'Bridal nerves, I expect. Perfectly normal.'

Angie didn't respond. What was normal about marrying a man you hated for the sole purpose of making him unhappy?

Suddenly submerged by a wave of panic, she was on the verge of withdrawing from the whole deal when she suddenly caught sight of her sister's photograph on the small table in the living room. Tiffany was laughing and posing, clearly flirting with the person behind the camera. Angie gave a soft, wistful smile and then felt a stab of pain. However foolish her sister had been, she hadn't deserved Nikos Kyriacou. She hadn't deserved to be so badly treated.

Staring at the photograph, she blinked back tears. If she didn't go through with the wedding then it would be someone else's sister. Someone else's loved one who was hurt. And she wasn't going to let him do it to anyone else.

'You look amazing.' The make-up artist was obviously trying to be reassuring. 'Your skin is so good you don't actually need much make-up. And you have an amazing bone structure. If you were a few inches taller you could find work as a model.'

Angie bit back the instinctive denial that leapt to her lips. The girl was trying to be kind, she reminded herself. And it was very sweet of her. It would be churlish to point out that she knew she looked absolutely nothing like a model.

'Thank you.'

'And I love your dress. Fabulous. It's simple but it really shows off your figure.'

Angie opened her mouth to say, What figure? but stopped herself in time, instead glancing down at the simple shift dress she'd chosen with a doubtful frown. It had been the first thing on the rail with a reasonably high neck. She certainly wouldn't have described it as fabulous. But she'd had to purchase something. It had crossed her mind that she might turn up at the wedding wearing her everyday navy suit just to irritate Nikos, but she had a nasty feeling that he was more than capable of stripping it off her and, anyway, she mused as she turned sideways and studied her reflection in the mirror, she wasn't prepared to wear navy to her wedding, even if the whole thing was a sham.

'Angelina—' Her mother entered the room and gave a soft

gasp. Wearing a dress of soft blue silk, she floated across to Angie and studied her in amazement. 'My goodness, you look almost—almost—'

'Thanks, Mum,' Angie interrupted her hastily before her mother could say something that would dent her fragile confidence.

'I mean you'll never touch Tiffany for looks, but at least you look tidy.' Her mother looked at the make-up artist and her eyes filled. 'My Tiffany was a real stunner.' She opened her bag and pulled out a handkerchief.

'No crying, Mum,' Angie said quickly, aware that the make-up artist was looking at them in amazement.

'I can't actually believe you're going through with this.' Her mother blew her nose. 'It's the *perfect* revenge. So clever. Not only does the man have to marry even though he doesn't want to but he has to marry *you*! And all I can say is he deserves it!'

'Thanks, Mum.' Her dry tone received no acknowledgement from her mother and Angie gave a sigh and quickly paid the make-up artist and hurried her out of the house, not even daring to imagine what must have been going on in the woman's head. Not only had it been made brutally clear to her that Angie's mother had an extremely low opinion of her own daughter, but she was obviously under the impression that Angie herself had trapped some poor unsuspecting male into marriage against his will.

Which was exactly what she *had* done, of course.

Feeling more and more jittery and less and less confident and sincerely wishing she'd agreed to meet her mother at the register office so that she wouldn't have been in a position to consistently undermine her when what she really needed was encouragement, Angie picked up her bag. 'Are you ready to leave? The car should be outside by now.'

'Of course I'm ready.' Her mother adjusted her hat and swept through the door. 'I want to see that man get his comeuppance. I want him walking down the aisle knowing that because he let Tiffany slip through his fingers he's now stuck with you.'

'It's a register office, Mum,' Angie reminded her patiently as she picked up her keys and locked the front door. 'We're not walking down an aisle. Nikos didn't want to do it in church.'

'Whatever.' Her mother's dismissive wave of her hand indicated that she considered the venue to be irrelevant. 'The contrast between you and your sister is so enormous that he's going to be *kicking* himself.'

Angie rolled her eyes. It was a good job that given the choice between beauty and brains she would have chosen brains. Otherwise her mother's comments would have made her too self-conscious to leave the house. But then, she'd had years to get used to it.

Nikos prowled the length of the tiny room and back again, ignoring the nervous glances of his bodyguard, who had already made the unfortunate *faux pas* of congratulating his employer on his wedding day. Reminded of something that he was trying hard to forget, Nikos had exploded in a tirade of Greek that had left his staff in no doubt at all as to his attitude to the institution of matrimony.

Aware that they would now all be wondering whether he'd made some poor unfortunate girl pregnant and been trapped into a hasty wedding, Nikos ground his teeth and paced the length of the room once more, battling an almost overwhelming urge to put his fist through the wall. He eyed the cheap chairs and plastic flowers with incredulous disbelief and no small degree of self-loathing. What the hell was he doing here? This was just the sort of situation that he'd successfully avoided all his life.

He'd decided many years before that marriage wasn't going to be for him, that commitment to one woman was best avoided. And now here he was; not only forced to marry, but forced to marry someone who would have been as far from his ideal choice of woman as it was possible to be.

The only glimmer of light on the horizon was that she obviously had no idea what she was letting herself in for. She'd clearly expected to be able to grab an indecent amount of money out of their wedding and he almost smiled as he contemplated the depth of her disappointment when she realised that the pre-nuptial agreement had been constructed in such a way as to ensure that she received not a single penny on their eventual divorce. And she obviously had some twisted belief that, by forcing him into a commitment that he'd previously avoided, she was going to punish him. Her naïvety was almost amusing. The truth was that he was so angry with the entire Littlewood family that he was actually beginning to relish the prospect of turning the tables on her.

If she was looking for a fight, then she'd come to the right place, he mused grimly, reflecting on the fact that Dr Angelina Littlewood was about to face a vastly superior adversary.

In the circumstances he found her continued defence of her sister distinctly unpalatable and, although he'd always considered himself to be an emotionally restrained person, he could no longer think about Tiffany without feeling his temper rise to dangerous levels. Having met the mother, it was obvious that she was a drunken version of her younger daughter and, as for the elder—

The door opened and Angie Littlewood stumbled through the door, wobbly on unfamiliar heels and clutching a small bunch of roses in front of her. Behind her, Gaynor Littlewood hovered, wearing a completely ridiculous hat, but Nikos didn't spare her a glance. His gaze was fixed on his bride-to-be.

He'd braced himself for the navy trouser suit and the usual haphazard hair. What he hadn't expected was a stylish dress in a soft fabric that skimmed her figure and hinted at feminine curves concealed beneath. His gaze lifted and lingered on her full lips, now accentuated by a subtle sheen of gloss and then settled on her hair, which had been swept on top of her head in an elegant knot.

She cast a quick glance around the room and walked over to him with exaggerated care, clearly trying not to trip on her shoes. 'You chose a small register office wedged between a public library and a supermarket in a small provincial town. One has to wonder why.' Clutching a small bouquet of roses, her blue eyes were cool as she looked up at him.

'Why not?' Nikos examined the freckles on her nose and wondered whether she had them anywhere else on her body. Suddenly in the grip of a vicious attack of lust, he almost laughed at himself. Why, when faced with a woman designed to drive carnal thoughts from a man's head, was he struggling with a massive erection? All right, so she had possibilities but he'd known that almost from the start. Some time between the removal of her glasses and the escape of her hair, he'd realised that Angie Littlewood had certain attractions—*attractions of which she, herself, appeared to be unaware*. But he knew better than anyone that sex was about so much more than the physical. He liked his women to be sophisticated, his equal sexually. He already had evidence that Angie's definition of 'erotic' involved all the passion of a business presentation. He wouldn't have been surprised to discover that she was a virgin. Realising that she was waiting for an answer to her question about the venue, he shrugged. 'Why not here?'

'It just isn't the sort of place I'd associate with a man like you.'

'Precisely.' He didn't even try to keep the impatience out of his tone. She might be an academic, but surely she wasn't that naïve? 'I, for one, am keen to avoid any sort of publicity. If the media discovered I was getting married, we would have been mobbed. I'm sure you wouldn't want that any more than I do.'

'Oh, yes, sorry. I'd forgotten how obsessed you are with your image.' She glanced at the bodyguard. 'You have no family here to celebrate with you?'

Ignoring her dig about image and determined to ignore the insidious throb in his loins, Nikos narrowed his eyes. 'What is there to celebrate?'

'You mean that you're ashamed of me.'

'I mean that I want the Brandizi diamond returned to my family and this appears to be the only way to secure that objective.'

He saw the faint flush on her cheeks and wondered for a moment whether he was seeing guilt. Then he reminded himself that she was a Littlewood and was betraying all the greed and money-grabbing tendencies that had characterised her sister's behaviour.

The registrar cleared her throat and Nikos watched as something akin to panic flashed in Angie's eyes.

'Last-minute nerves, *agape mou*?' He leaned forward, his eyes gentle as he lifted a hand and brushed her cheek in what appeared to those watching to be an affectionate gesture. 'My dear, sweet Angelina.' His lips brushed her skin and he lowered his voice, the rest of his words for her ears only. 'Enjoy your last moments as a single, independent woman. You're about to become my property.'

CHAPTER SIX

EVERY minute of the brief civil ceremony was agonising and, as soon as it was over, Angie escaped from the oppressive heat of the register office and took refuge on the pavement, breathing in gulps of cool air. Despite the fact that it was June, the sky was ominously grey and it was now raining steadily. All around her Saturday shoppers grappled with umbrellas and jostled each other, laughing together and hurrying with bags stuffed with goods, anxious to escape the damp weather.

Ignoring the rain, Angie watched them with envy, wondering whether she could make a run for it and lose herself in their midst. Her life had been simple once. Her life had been—

'Angelina!' Nikos strode out of the building, flanked by two bodyguards and Angie straightened her spine, ready for the inevitable conflict.

'*Don't* call me Angelina.'

He stopped in front of her, powerful shoulders encased in a dark, expensive suit, his features hard and cold but so indecently handsome that passing women walked into puddles ankle deep because they were so busy gaping at him. 'I can call you anything I like. You're my wife.' His lingering emphasis on those two little words made her shiver.

'That doesn't give you any rights.'

'That's where you're wrong.' He smiled and closed strong fingers around her wrist. 'It gives me all the rights I need, *agape mou*. Give me the jewel.'

She hesitated. 'Can I wear it a little longer? It's just that I—it—' *It reminded her of her sister.*

'I need the jewel back and I need it now. It is, after all, the reason I married you.'

Unable to argue with him, she lifted her hands to the back of her neck and released the clasp that held the pendant round her neck. 'It seemed the safest place for it.'

He gave a derisory smile as he took the pendant from her and handed it to one of his bodyguards. 'Given the likelihood that few men have been given access to that area of your body, I'm forced to agree with you. And now I need to leave.'

Angie's eyes were still on the jewel and she felt a lump building in her throat. Letting it go shouldn't make a difference. *She really shouldn't mind.* 'Leave?'

'I've already spent far too much time in this rain-soaked country.' He glanced around him with distaste. 'I have urgent business problems in Greece which require my personal attention.'

Finally his words sank in. He was leaving?

It was the best news she'd had for a long time. 'Fine. Off you go, then. I've given you the jewel. We have no more to say to one another.' Weak with relief at the prospect of his abrupt departure, Angie allowed herself a brief fantasy of an evening spent in the library, reading an ancient text.

'You really think I'd consider travelling without my bride?' His voice silky-smooth, he yanked her up against him and moulded her against his lean, hard frame. 'We're newly married, *agape mou*. We are supposed to spend time together. Indulge each other's deepest and wildest fantasies. Wasn't that your intention when you begged me to marry you?'

'I didn't beg you to marry me, at least not in the way you're suggesting.' The shock of his body so intimately pressed against hers caused her heart to thunder and her stomach to perform a series of acrobatic manoeuvres. 'My intention was to curb your womanising, which I've successfully achieved.' She tried to wriggle away from his hold but he held her easily. 'You're not allowed to be seen within a million miles of another woman for the next two years. That's punishment enough for a man like you. I'll stay here and you can go back to Greece and start your sentence.'

'I'm afraid it doesn't work that way.' His tone sympathetic, he released her briefly but only to sweep her into his arms and drop her unceremoniously on to the back seat of the waiting car. 'Where I go, you go. That's what marriage and commitment is all about. Togetherness.'

She gave a gasp and tried to climb back out of the car but the doors were locked and she turned to him in outrage. 'Unlock the doors.'

'The car is already moving,' he pointed out gently. 'If I unlock the doors you will end up having a serious accident, which I can't permit. You see, I don't have time to take you to the hospital and have you patched up. I need you, alive and in one piece.'

Her hand still on the door handle, she stared at him. There was something in his tone that made her nervous. 'What do you mean, you "need me"?'

'The words should be relatively easy to understand by someone of your reputed intelligence.'

'You can't possibly need me.'

He flicked some dust from the sleeve of his immaculate and undoubtedly ferociously expensive suit. 'I'm afraid the woman in my life is expected to perform a certain number of functions. I do a great deal of corporate entertaining.'

'I'm sure you do.' She let go of the door handle. 'But I'm also sure you employ staff.'

'Sixty thousand across the globe at the last count.'

He employed that many people? Hiding her shock, she turned away with a casual shrug. 'Then I'm sure that at least one of those sixty thousand would jump at the chance of helping you with your entertaining.'

'Without a doubt, but that isn't permitted, is it?' His voice was a soft, lethal purr. 'You made me sign a clause which prevents me from ever being seen with another woman. The problem is that I *need* a woman in my life to fulfil certain vital functions and the only woman I'm allowed to be seen with is you. So you're going to have to do it.'

She turned to look at him. 'By "certain vital functions", you're talking about hospitality.'

'That's one need, certainly.' He inclined his dark head and his eyes glittered dangerously. 'But not the main one.'

She rolled her eyes. 'So what's the main one?'

'Stress relief.' He suppressed a yawn and settled back in his seat, clearly starting to enjoy himself.

He didn't appear in the slightest bit stressed, unlike Angie, who was feeling the tension in the air growing by the minute. 'You're saying that you need female company to relax?'

'I'm saying that I need *sex* to relax, *agape mou.*' He loosened his tie with a casual flick of long bronzed fingers. 'The greater the pressure in my working life, the more sex I need and I probably ought to warn you that I've got some pretty major deals going on at the moment.'

Shock made the breath catch in her throat and there was something in his penetrating masculine gaze that made her feel distinctly odd inside. She'd never met a man as overtly sexual as Nikos Kyriacou. Even an expensive designer suit couldn't disguise the slightly rough, basic aura that surrounded him. 'The pre-nuptial agreement prevents you from seeing other women.'

'I know.' He gave her a sympathetic smile and dropped the tie on to the seat next to him. 'You're probably going to be completely exhausted, but I am pretty busy at work during the day so hopefully you'll be able to catch up on some sleep while I'm in the office.'

She froze. 'Why would I need to sleep while you're in the office?'

'Because I intend to keep you up all night,' he said helpfully, his tone matter-of-fact.

Her pulse rate trebled with no warning. 'You're saying that you need sex,' she said stiffly, managing not to stumble over the word, 'but you should have thought of that before you broke my sister's heart.'

His gaze was slumberous. '*You* should have thought of that before you restricted my access to other women, *agape mou*. I'm not capable of doing without sex. So I'm just going to have to make do with you.'

She gave a muted gasp. 'You're joking.'

'I never joke about sex. I find it an extremely serious subject. Without sex I'm incredibly irritable. You wouldn't like me.'

Her heart was pounding with rhythmic force. 'I don't like you now.' She licked dry lips, aware of a growing heat low in her pelvis. 'The whole point of this deal was to make you suffer. You're going to have to learn to be celibate.'

'Unfortunately there are certain words that just don't appear in my vocabulary and "celibate" is definitely one of them.' He stifled a yawn. 'I'm not that great with "failure" or "impoverished" either and "no" has always presented me with significant problems, but I'm working on that one in certain circumstances. For example, if you were to ask me if I can do without sex then the answer is most definitely going to be "no".'

His mocking tone infuriated her and she shifted to the edge of her seat, her whole body tense. 'If you think I'd even contemplate going to bed with you, then you don't know me at all.'

'Well, sex will soon solve that. It's an excellent way of getting to know someone. And actually, I know quite a bit about you.' His gaze dropped to her mouth and then lifted. 'You don't even recognise the basic signs of sexual attraction, do you?'

She stiffened and gripped the seat tightly, wishing that she was better equipped to give a smooth put-down. 'If you're asking whether I find you attractive, then I've already told you that I don't. I'm sorry if that hurts your feelings, but it's the truth.'

'You find me unbelievably attractive, that's the truth.'

Before she could compose a suitable reply, the car door opened and Nikos gestured with his hand. 'We need to move or I'll be late for my meeting.'

She hadn't even realised that the car had stopped and she stared in surprise at the large aeroplane on the runway. 'What's that?'

'It's an aeroplane,' Nikos said helpfully, reaching across and bodily removing her from the back of the car. 'It's fuelled and ready for take-off once the passengers are on board.'

'The passengers?' Clutching her bag, she stood on the runway, staring at the huge aircraft.

'Your questions are extremely entertaining but if I answer them all now I'll never make my meeting. Make a list and we can go through them later.' Without further attempt at conversation, Nikos snapped his fingers at his security team and then locked his fingers round Angie's wrist and strode towards the steps.

'Wait a minute.' She tugged at her arm. 'I can't leave the country. My life is here. My job. My mother isn't well—'

'We both know that your mother received an instant cure to her ills the day she realised that her daughter was marrying a billionaire,' he said dryly, not slackening his stride. 'She was looking in radiant health this morning. Unlike you, who were as white as a snowdrift.'

Unable to refute his comment about her mother, Angie bit her lip. 'I'm naturally pale—it goes with my hair colour—and you don't seem to understand. I have a job at the Museum and I lecture at the University.'

'You should have thought of those things before you blackmailed me into marrying you.'

The word made her distinctly uneasy. 'I didn't blackmail you.'

'No?' They'd reached the bottom of the steps and he paused for a moment, dragging her against him with a ruthless sense of purpose. 'If I don't marry you, I don't get the jewel. What's that if it isn't blackmail?'

Hating the sound of the word, she stared into his glittering dark eyes and felt nerves flicker inside her. 'All right—' her voice cracked slightly '—I'm willing to admit that I might have overreacted slightly. I was *very* upset about my sister and you are *so* unfeeling, which didn't help at all.' She eyed the steps of the aircraft, suddenly facing the enormity of what she'd done. 'But I can't go to Greece. I can't go with you. So we'll just forget the whole thing. You can have the jewel and I'll divorce you and—'

'Giving up so easily, Angelina?' His voice was silky-smooth. 'I thought you wanted to punish me? This is going to be no fun at all if you don't at least *try* to be a worthy adversary.'

She *did* want to punish him, but suddenly he seemed to be the one in control. They were about to board *his* plane to go to *his* country.

How had it happened? One minute she'd been making the demands and the next he'd taken over.

Trying to be something she wasn't just didn't work, she

thought miserably as she struggled for an escape route. He'd goaded her into being angry and vengeful but the feelings hadn't lasted because that wasn't the sort of person she was. She hadn't been thinking straight and she hadn't been able to bear the thought of parting with the jewel. But now she just felt foolish and out of her depth.

'We'll just get divorced,' she muttered, tugging at her hand. 'I'll see a lawyer this afternoon and sort something out.'

'Don't waste your time. My lawyer is the best there is. There won't be any way out of this marriage until the two years that you stipulated are up.' His fingers tightened around her wrist, removing any thoughts she might have had of making a run for it. 'It's a pity for both of us that you didn't have your second thoughts a few weeks ago. As it is, there are no loopholes in the contract we signed. For better or for worse, we have to endure each other's company for the next two years. Make the best of it.'

'But—'

'If you're going to argue, would you mind doing it on board? My pilot's ready to take off and I don't want us to miss our slot.' With that he propelled her up the steps towards the door of the aircraft, giving her no opportunity for further argument.

Bemused and uncertain, she stumbled into the aircraft and stopped dead, blinking with shock. She'd expected rows of seats, all facing forwards with no leg room, but the reality was totally different.

It was like being inside an extremely elegant living room. Deep leather sofas faced each other across a deeply carpeted aisle, inviting the occupant to curl up and relax. Further down inside the aircraft was a large round table able to seat at least twenty in comfort, and beyond that were several doors.

'Kitchen, bedroom, bathroom and cinema,' Nikos drawled

in a bored tone, nudging her inside and on to one of the sofas. 'Put a seat belt on or my pilot gets anxious.'

'Your pilot?'

'You're doing it again,' he pointed out gently as he took a pile of papers from one of the four flight attendants who were hovering. 'Asking questions. Tiana?'

'Yes, sir?' The blonde flight attendant who had given him the papers stepped forward, her manner discreet and respectful.

'We're going to need to eat and then I want a conference call with Christian and Dimitri.' He signed the papers with a bold, confident sweep of his hand and gave them back to her.

'Yes, sir.' The girl took the papers and gave Angie a smile. 'Welcome on board. If there's anything at all you need, please ask.'

Angie suppressed the almost hysterical desire to laugh. Glancing round the enormous interior, she felt like asking for a map. She'd never been on a plane that looked like this one before. In fact, she'd seen apartments smaller than this plane.

'Is it yours?'

Nikos glanced up from the remaining papers, his dark brows locked in an impatient frown. 'Is what mine?'

'This plane.' She swallowed and rubbed a foot over the thick carpeting.

'Of course.' The expression on his face told her a great deal about what he thought of her question and she blushed slightly, wondering how her sister could have had the confidence to move in these circles. She felt *totally* out of her depth.

'Why can't you just fly in a normal plane like everyone else?'

'I'm not everyone else.' He put the papers down in front of him and fastened his seat belt. 'I can't run a global business if I'm restricted by the schedule of a commercial airline.'

'So you have your own plane.'

'I have my own *fleet* of planes,' he corrected her gently.

'Five at the last count, so that all the members of my senior team are able to be mobile and still work while travelling. It makes commercial sense.' He reached out, took a glass of champagne from the flight attendant and handed it to her.

'I don't drink.'

'Then start,' he advised in a silky tone, placing the glass down on the table in front of her. 'It will help you relax and that would be a benefit for both of us. I find you *incredibly* uptight and tense, which does nothing for my stress levels.'

Something in the look in his slumberous dark eyes made her feel even more uneasy and she couldn't help but remember the conversation they'd had about his stress levels. *He'd said that he needed sex to relieve the tension.*

She looked away, so tense that she couldn't ever imagine being relaxed again. It was just *him*, she thought, sneaking a look at his handsome face as he switched from English to Greek to talk to the stewardess. He made her nervous. Looking at the stack of papers demanding his attention, she remembered his comment about needing an antidote to stress and gave a little shiver. He hadn't been serious about that, she told herself quickly. He just liked to make her feel as uncomfortable and embarrassed as possible.

But, all the same, she reached for the champagne and took a small sip, deciding that she needed the courage. She still couldn't quite believe that she was on her way to Greece but one glance out of the window directly opposite confirmed that they were high above the clouds.

Nikos rose to his feet to take the conference call and she was left to her own devices, listening with just one ear as the conversation conducted in rapid Greek turned from emerging markets to the rise in oil prices.

Being fluent in his language brought her no closer to understanding what he did, she thought wryly as she settled back in the sofa and picked up a magazine from the table by her elbow. She knew from Tiffany that he owned hotels and a shipping company but all the newspaper articles she'd read on him said that his genius lay in finance.

Resigned to the fact that his goals and interests were entirely foreign to her and were likely to remain that way, Angie scanned the magazine, ignoring an article on the latest fashion in beachwear in favour of a piece on the ancient site of Knossos on the island of Crete.

It was only when the plane eventually landed, more than four hours after they'd taken off from London, that she realised she hadn't even asked where in Greece they were going. After he'd finished his conference call, Nikos had settled himself on the sofa opposite and proceeded to work his way through an enormous pile of papers, occasionally signing his name, occasionally making notes in the margin.

'Are we on your island?'

Closing his briefcase and releasing his seat belt, Nikos rose in a fluid movement. 'The island doesn't have a runway big enough for a 747. We are on the island of Crete.'

She stared at him. 'You have a house on Crete?'

'A villa. When I'm not in New York or Tokyo, I commute between here and Athens during the week. I use the island at weekends and when I have a particular desire for privacy. Don't look so worried.' He handed the papers to the flight attendant, who took them and melted into the background. 'Crete is full of ancient sites and bits of broken pottery. You should feel right at home, Dr Kyriacou. If you develop withdrawal symptoms from the Museum, you can always go and dig in my garden.'

Ignoring the faint sarcasm in his voice, she followed him out of the aircraft, telling herself that maybe things weren't going to be so bad after all. Four hours closeted in an aeroplane with him had been enough to show her that he was a complete workaholic. He clearly couldn't stand the sight of her, which meant that she was going to be pretty much left to her own devices and what better place to be left alone than Crete, with its amazing history?

All she had to do was stay out of his way and everything would be fine.

They drove from the airport along the coast just as the sun started to set. Fingers of fire spread across the sea and in the distance mountains loomed, dark and mysterious. By the time the driver paused outside a set of large electric gates it was almost dark.

Nikos was talking into his phone again and Angie watched while the gates swung open and the car moved slowly up a long curving driveway illuminated by delicate lights. Glimpsing orange trees laden with fruit, she inched further forwards in her seat, enchanted. She wanted to get out of the car and explore but the drive seemed to go on for ever. Obviously Nikos Kyriacou valued his privacy, she thought dryly and was just wondering whether they were ever going to arrive when they took a final curve in the long driveway and pulled up outside the villa.

Feeling daunted, she followed him up the steps to the entrance. Inside, she paused in the hallway, her eyes immediately drawn to a pot, displayed on a simply designed table.

'Oh, my goodness—' As if in a trance, she stepped closer, lifted a hand as if to touch and then stopped herself. She turned to look at him, disbelief in her eyes. 'Is it—?'

'You tell me,' he drawled, stepping to one side as his staff hurried past him with luggage. 'You're the archaeologist.'

'It's early Minoan,' she breathed, turning her head again and running her eyes over the pot. 'An amphora—a storage jar. It's a fabulous piece.' She couldn't hide her surprise. 'I had no idea you were interested in archaeology. You never—'

'We haven't exactly had time to discuss our hobbies, have we?' The sardonic lift of his dark brow indicated exactly what he thought of her line in conversation. 'I'm Greek. All Greeks are interested in their heritage.'

But not all Greeks could afford artefacts of this rarity, she thought to herself. 'Do you have anything else?'

'You want me to show you my etchings?'

She made an impatient sound and turned away, flustered. 'It's impossible to conduct a conversation with you.'

'Good, because I've done nothing but talk all day and I need a rest from it. Are you hungry or do you want to go straight to bed?'

'Bed sounds good,' she muttered immediately, grateful that he'd given her the option of just retiring for the night. She was exhausted by the events of the day. Exhausted by him. Bed would provide a welcome sanctuary from his ice cold scrutiny and his sarcastic line in communication.

He took her hand in his and led her up the curving staircase towards the first floor. 'All the bedrooms have balconies overlooking the sea.' He flung open the first door and she gave a gasp of delight.

The heavy silk cover draped over the four-poster bed was scattered with pink rose petals, some of which had floated down on to the exquisite rug which covered the tiled floor. A wall of glass opened on to the balcony and she could hear the gentle sounds of the sea. 'It's stunning.'

He pushed the door shut with the palm of his hand, a frown on his handsome face as he noticed the bed. 'I'm afraid my staff occasionally get a little carried away.'

'I like it,' she said hastily, glancing towards the door. 'I'll be fine now, thanks. You don't have to stay.'

'Unfortunately, I do.' He lifted a hand and released the knot of his tie. 'I had a very stressful working day.'

She stared at him, her heart stumbling in her chest. 'You're not sleeping here.'

'That's right. I'm not. I'm far too wound up to sleep.' He strolled towards the window and dropped his tie over the back of the chair. Then he shrugged out of his jacket and slowly undid the buttons of his shirt while she watched, frozen to the spot. Surely he wasn't seriously intending to—

'I need a bath,' she said quickly, 'so don't wait around for me. You just go and do whatever it is you need to do to relax. Get changed and enjoy a glass of ouzo, take a dip in your pool—'

'I've already told you my favourite method of relaxation.' The shirt joined the tie and the jacket over the back of the chair and she quickly looked away, but not before she'd caught a graphic glimpse of bronzed, muscular chest covered in curling black hairs. 'But by all means freshen up. The bathroom is the door to your right.'

Grateful to have been offered an escape, she shot through it quickly and bolted it firmly behind her. He didn't mean it, she told herself firmly, trying to breathe slowly and calm her pounding heart. He was just joking about his favourite method of relaxation.

He wasn't interested in her. He'd made his opinion on that subject quite clear and that was fine because she didn't want his interest.

If necessary she'd stay in the bathroom until he'd had time to fall asleep.

Feeling in need of relaxation herself, she walked across the room and stared at the buttons on the wall, trying to work out how to run water into the enormous sunken bath. Still trying to work it out, she added some designer bath foam from the wide selection left in a pot and then experimented nervously with a few different knobs until a powerful jet of water shot out of the taps, filling the tub in seconds.

Even knowing that the locked door was between them, Angie still hesitated before pulling her dress over her head and slipping out of her underwear.

He was just trying to shock her, she thought to herself as she slid under the scented foam. *Trying to frighten and intimidate her.* He was angry because she had the upper hand. She'd forced him to be celibate—to think about his relationships.

Enjoying the feel of warm water and the delicious scent of the bath foam, she closed her eyes and started to feel a little better. The feeling lasted until she heard the distinct sound of a door opening.

Her eyes flew open and widened in shocked disbelief as Nikos strolled towards her dressed only in a pair of black silk boxer shorts. His shoulders were broad and bare, his legs long and well muscled and he was the epitome of prime manhood.

'I locked the door.' Her voice was a horrified squeak and he gave a careless shrug.

'There are two doors, *agape mou*. Evidently you didn't lock both of them.'

CHAPTER SEVEN

'GET out.' Even though the bubbles covered her completely, she slid deeper under the water, her voice an outraged squeak. 'I want privacy.'

'You should have thought of that before you proposed marriage and imposed no end of restrictions on my lifestyle.' Without a flicker of hesitation or modesty, he slid his boxer shorts off and joined her in the bath.

Shocked by such a blatant display of manhood, her immediate instinct was to shoot out of the water but that would have meant parading naked in front of him and she didn't have sufficient confidence in her body.

Unlike him.

He obviously had no qualms whatsoever about stripping naked in front of her. He hadn't even turned sideways or attempted to cover his modesty with a towel. He was a vision of bronzed, muscular perfection—a tough, athletic male whose claim that he needed sex was supported by the unmistakable power of his extremely large erection.

Deciding that parading naked was less daunting than remaining in the bath with him, she eyed the pile of soft fluffy towels but, before she could make a dash for it, she felt his hand clamp around her wrist.

'You can't—'

'Yes, I can.' Without further argument, he pulled her across his lap. She squirmed and tried to stand up but the bubbles had made the water slippery and anyway he was much, much stronger than her. She wriggled again but then felt the hard thrust of his erection against her thigh and froze. Her eyes met his and saw humour there, along with an emotion far more primal and basic.

'Sorry, but I did warn you,' he murmured softly as he slid an arm round her waist and brought his mouth down on hers.

The touch of his lips sent a bolt of fire through her pelvis and she gave a gasp of shock which turned to a moan of disbelief as his tongue slid between her parted lips and he kissed her with a degree of erotic expertise that she'd never before encountered.

She felt the rough scrape of male stubble against her face, felt the hardness of his thighs under hers and then her eyes drifted shut and she was transported into a different word, a sensual world where thoughts no longer mattered. Where feelings were the only thing that counted.

The warm scented water lapped around her, his mouth moved seductively over hers and then she felt the strength and pressure of his hand at her waist, urging her closer. Her hand rested on his chest and she felt the steady beat of his heart under her fingers as she dizzily tried to remember why this situation didn't feel entirely right.

But, before she could make an attempt at rational thought, his fingers brushed across her nipple and she gave a cry of shock. Excitement stabbed hard through her body and she squirmed against his hard thighs, trying to ease the sudden nagging ache deep inside her.

Without lifting his mouth from hers, he dragged his fingers over her nipple again, this time repeating the caress until she could stand it no longer and dragged her lips from his so that she could gasp in some much needed air.

She heard him mutter something in Greek, something that she didn't understand, and then he buried his face in her neck and she threw back her head with a low moan as she felt the hot brand of his mouth burning her bare skin. Her whole body was on fire, shivering and burning with need, and she felt the leisurely slide of his hand from waist to hip, felt him move her slightly and then felt the confident stroke of his strong fingers close to the heart of her femininity.

She gave a half-hearted wriggle in an attempt to protect herself but she was weakened and dizzy and he simply parted her thighs with a gentle but decisive movement of his hands and then she felt the intimate probe of his touch as he slid a finger deep inside her.

It felt so deliciously good that she gasped in shock, her vision blurred as she clutched at the hard muscle of his shoulder, her whole body trembling and tense, everything focused on the clever stroke of his fingers. Deep down she knew she ought to resist but she had no idea how to stop him, had no idea how to subdue the wicked sensations that threatened to consume her body.

Her breathing shallow, her fingers dug into his arm. Then his mouth found hers again and his tongue traced her lips in an exploration so shockingly sexual that the throb in her pelvis intensified to almost intolerable levels.

Lost in the devastation of his kiss, she was dimly aware of the skilled, knowing movement of his fingers but she couldn't work out what he was doing because his touch seemed to be everywhere and it felt impossibly, maddeningly good. Her body felt different, everything felt different, and she moaned against his mouth and squirmed against his hand, desperate for something, but she didn't know exactly what. But he seemed to know exactly what she needed because he continued his relentless assault on her senses until she felt her body suddenly explode in a shower of sensation and felt herself tighten around his seeking fingers.

Shaken and weak from the experience, she dragged her mouth away from his and buried her face in his shoulder, far too embarrassed to look at him. Now that some of the unbelievable tension had eased, she felt incredibly shy but he didn't give her a chance to hide because he rose to his feet with her still in his arms, yanked a warm towel from the pile and strode through to the bedroom.

'Nikos—' her voice was strangled and shaking with embarrassment '—I'm dripping on the carpet. I'm naked— please, just let me—'

'I don't care about the carpet and you don't need to tell me that you're naked,' he drawled softly, dropping the towel on to the centre of the bed and lowering her on top of it. 'I can feel that you're naked. I've had you rubbing against me for the best part of an hour.'

An hour? She stared up at him in disbelief. Had it really been that long?

The knowledge that so much time had passed and she hadn't even noticed left her even more embarrassed. But nothing was more embarrassing than lying naked with him poised above her, his gaze roaming freely over her body.

She tried to cover herself but he caught her arms and gave a faint smile.

'A bit late for modesty,' he said huskily, 'since I'm already intimately acquainted with your body.'

Riddled with insecurities about herself, she tried to roll away from him but he shifted in a smooth movement and came down on top of her and she gasped.

'Why are you doing this? You know I'm not your sort of woman—'

'At this precise moment you're *exactly* my sort of woman,' he assured her in heavily accented tones as he lowered his mouth to within a breath of hers. 'You're damp, naked and still a bit weak after your first orgasm. Speaking as a man, it doesn't get much better than this.'

Shock mingled with another far more dangerous emotion as she felt the bold thrust of his arousal against her thigh. She tried to use the last of her logic before it deserted her. 'I'm overweight and I don't know anything about sex.'

'I know enough for both of us,' he assured her arrogantly, his hand sliding slowly down the length of her body as if to prove his point. 'And you're *not* overweight. You have fabulous breasts. You feel soft and womanly and very, very tempting, *agape mou.*'

His voice alone was a seduction and she forgot that no man had ever spoken to her in such a way and found herself closing her eyes as the same delicious heat started to spread through her lower body. She didn't want this, but she couldn't resist.

'Open your eyes.' His soft command cut through the haze in her brain and she did as he ordered and then wished she hadn't because there was something in his dangerous dark gaze that made her shiver. He was the ultimate male animal, king of the beasts surveying his chosen mate.

And he'd chosen to seduce her.

'This time I want to watch your expression.' His eyes held hers and then he rolled away from her body and lay on his side, his eyes drifting slowly down every quivering inch of her body. 'I can't believe you cover such an amazing body under those awful clothes.'

She gazed at him, vulnerability in her eyes. 'I don't really think about what I wear,' she confessed, wondering why talking felt so difficult. 'I know I'll never be beautiful so I don't try.'

'Clever and beautiful,' he murmured, his hand lingering on the fullness of her breast.

She knew there was nothing amazing or beautiful about her body but the heat of his gaze burned away the last of her insecurities. A small part of her mind was trying to tell her that she shouldn't be doing this, that this wasn't what was supposed to have happened between them, but the rest of her mind was completely taken over by the crash course in sensuality that he was currently giving her.

He bent his head to her breast and flicked a tongue over her nipple and hot needles of sharp excitement pierced the length of her body. She squirmed under him and sank her fingers into his glossy dark hair as he continued to subject her to a continuous assault on her senses that left her shaking and barely able to breathe.

'Nikos—I don't—I can't—You have to stop—' Unable to believe that she could feel like this again, she arched against him in an instinctive feminine invitation and he lifted his head reluctantly.

'Stop?' His words were slightly slurred and his jaw was dark with stubble. He looked wickedly handsome and arrogantly male. 'Why would I stop?'

'Because we really shouldn't—'

'You're my wife.' He slid a hand over the gentle curve of her stomach. 'So we absolutely should.' His hand moved lower still and she tensed slightly as she felt his touch grow more intimate.

'Oh—' She felt him slide a leisurely finger deep inside her and she gave a shiver that intensified as he withdrew his finger and gently, skilfully, drew the tip over the moist nub of her femininity.

Exquisite pleasure shot through her and she closed her eyes and gave a sharp cry that she was helpless to hold back.

Murmuring something in Greek, he spread her legs wide and slid his mouth down her body, opening her and exposing her to the skilled flick of his tongue.

She felt the heat of his breath against her and tried to close her legs but he ignored her feeble attempts and held her wide, allowing himself the access he needed. And within seconds she forgot about modesty and thought only about satisfaction. The lower half of her body burned and ached as he slowly, deliberately drew his tongue over her most sensitive place. She felt his fingers slide back inside her, felt the building pressure inside her body and then everything exploded inside her and her body tightened around his fingers. Her climax throbbed relentlessly, refusing to release her from its agonizing grip, and she sobbed his name and begged him to stop but his tongue coaxed and teased and explored until one orgasm merged into another. For the first time in her life, the entire focus of her world was sensual pleasure and when the explosion and aftershocks finally subsided she lay limp and breathless, eyes closed.

Slowly her heart rate slowed and her breathing approached normal. Then she felt him move upwards and claim her mouth with his.

His kiss was slow and explicitly sexual, an echo of the intimacy that they'd just shared, and she was suddenly aware that his fingers were still buried deep inside her.

'You feel amazing, *agape mou*,' he said huskily as he lifted his mouth from hers and shifted his powerful body over hers, removing his fingers with a slow, deliberate movement that revealed just how well he understood her body. 'And now I think you understand the true meaning of the word "erotic", you're ready to take it all a stage further.' With masculine purpose and a total lack of inhibition, he slid an arm under her, positioned her exactly as he wanted and thrust hard into her still quivering body.

Plunged from one maelstrom of sexual discovery straight into another, Angie felt him lift her hips and pump with rhythmic force, his dark eyes glittering in his handsome face as he lowered his head and slid his tongue between her lips in a kiss as basic and carnal as the rest of his lovemaking.

She could concentrate on nothing except his body and how it fitted with hers. She felt the thickness and size of his erection, felt his body demand and take, felt hers yield and offer up all that she had to give. He allowed her no escape, no place to hide as he thrust into her again and again, driving them both to a state of suspended desperation.

With a grunt of male satisfaction he slid his fingers into her hair and tightened his grip and she felt everything inside her build to such an intense level that she scraped her nails down his back and arched against him in an instinctive demand for fulfilment.

'I want you to come again,' he breathed against her mouth, his words a dark, sultry command. 'You are going to let yourself go and give me everything that you are. I don't want you to hold anything back, Angelina.'

His seductive masculine tone barely registered because the demands of her body had long since taken over from her mind as the ruling force. She was so desperate, *so frantic for respite from the almost vicious throb of sexual desire*, that she was willing to do anything, anything, just to reach that point that her body instinctively craved.

With a low murmur of encouragement he shifted the angle of his body, raised her hips higher and thrust hard into her silken sheath. The throb became concentrated on just that one part and she felt her body explode around the solid force of his erection, heard him mutter something harsh in Greek and then knew that he had reached the same peak.

She dug her nails into his shoulder, sure that she was going to die—sure that it wasn't possible to survive such a protracted explosion of pleasure.

When the delicious spasms finally died away she lay limp and exhausted, too drained to think, let alone speak. She was dimly aware of his weight on her, dimly aware of his harsh breathing and the slick heat of his skin, but she wasn't able to move. She lay there with her eyes closed, sobbing for breath. 'I've never—I didn't know—'

'I thought you said that you weren't a virgin?'

'I wasn't.' Her eyes opened then and she stared at him with a dreamy expression. 'I mean I have—but it wasn't—I didn't know it could be like that. That was amazing.' Following an impulse that she didn't understand, she slid her arms round his neck and hugged him. For a moment she thought he was going to hug her back and then she felt him tense and pull away.

'It was sex,' he supplied helpfully, withdrawing from her and rolling on to his back. 'Glad to know I exceeded your expectations.'

His words jarred, rasped against the soft, lazy tenderness she felt growing inside her.

Suddenly cold, she gave a shiver and reached for the sheet to cover herself, but a lean bronzed hand reached down and stopped her.

'*Don't* cover up.' His eyes held no trace of affection. 'When you're in my bed, you're naked. That's one of my rules.'

How could he be so hard after the intimacy they'd just shared? How could he know so little about her when he'd just discovered so much? What had she done? 'I can't relax if I'm naked,' she said in a low voice and he stifled a yawn.

'Then learn.'

She swallowed, wishing she could be as confident about her body as he clearly was with his own. Unlike her, he made no attempt to cover himself. He was entirely comfortable, almost arrogant, in his nakedness and it was hardly surprising. His body would have been the envy of the most narcissistic Greek god.

Despite her best intentions, her gaze slid down from his broad shoulders. Dark body hair tangled across his broad chest, his abdomen was flat and a trail of hair led the way to the proud jut of his erection. He was arrogantly masculine and the fact that he was still hard brought another rush of colour to her cheeks.

He followed the direction of her gaze, registered her response and gave a faint smile. 'I need lots of sex. I think I already warned you about that. You're going to be extremely busy, *agape mou.*'

Remembering all the things he'd done to her, all the things she'd allowed him to do, she suddenly felt ridiculously shy and would have looked away but he caught her chin in his strong fingers, forcing her to meet his burning dark gaze. 'Don't look away from me. I don't want the archaeologist in my bed, Angelina, I want the woman.' Having delivered that statement, he shifted slightly so that his mouth hovered close to hers. 'Outside my bed you can spend all the time you wish examining pots and bones and reading ancient dusty books. But here, between the sheets in my bed, I want nothing but flesh and blood. Remember that.'

She felt cold and hot at the same time, her mind rejecting his words even as her traitorous body flared with excitement. Without the potent drug of seduction to cloud her senses, she was all too aware of exactly what she'd done. *And whom she'd done it with.* She couldn't help but be aware of the comparisons he must be making with Tiffany, who'd been so blonde and perfect. She felt so guilty that she'd been intimate with the man whom her sister had loved so deeply.

'We shouldn't have done that.' It had been some sort of twisted revenge on his part.

His smile was wry. 'Fortunately the body is not as discerning as the mind. And I have to admit that it proved to be surprisingly erotic having a woman who knows everything there is to know about pottery in the classical era and absolutely nothing about her own body. You were an astonishingly responsive and gratifying pupil. Everything I did to you, you just wanted more.'

She found his blatant reminder of the way she'd begged and clung to him intensely humiliating. 'I don't want to talk about it.'

'Good, because neither do I. Talking about it is never quite as much fun as *doing* it.' He sprang out of bed and strolled over to the bathroom. 'You can go to sleep if you like. I'll let you know when I want you again.'

Shocked by his gross lack of sensitivity after what they'd shared, she gave a soft gasp and sat up, her hair sliding over her shoulders in soft waves. If she needed any evidence that it hadn't been special to him then she had it now. 'You're completely heartless, do you know that?' She tried to keep the hurt from her voice but she knew she hadn't succeeded. 'I honestly don't know what my sister saw in you.'

'You're supposed to be intelligent. Rack your brains and I'm sure something will come to you.'

Her spine straightened. 'If you're suggesting that Tiffany was only interested in you for your money,' she said stiffly, 'then you're even crueller and more cynical than I thought. She liked nice things, of course she did, but she was in love with you.'

His dark eyes flashed a warning. 'Another rule—we don't discuss your sister in this bedroom. *Ever.*'

'But—'

'If you really don't wish to sleep, then I can think of other far more satisfying ways of passing the night than talking.'

The questions froze on her tongue and she flopped back on the bed and turned sideways, curling her legs up in an instinctive gesture of self-protection.

How could she have thought she'd seen gentleness in his eyes? He was incapable of feeling anything for anyone.

No woman had ever hugged him like that before.

Nikos stood under the shower, wrestling with entirely unfamiliar emotions. For the first time in his life, he felt unsettled, uncomfortable and—guilty?

What was the matter with him?

Leaving an extremely beautiful woman exhausted and satisfied in his bed was a common occurrence. Having hot sex with a woman who clearly wanted more from him was another common occurrence. He was used to dealing with women's dreamy and entirely unrealistic expectations, used to disentangling himself from the potential threat of commitment. He was careful never to use the word 'love' and careful not to display affection which might be misinterpreted. So far his strategy had worked. He made his rules perfectly clear right up front and relationships with women had never caused him a problem.

Until now.

Closing his eyes, he let the water wash over him.

Why should his encounter with Angelina have left him feeling guilty?

One hug didn't change the fact that she was a gold-digging opportunist who had seen a way of landing herself a billionaire lifestyle. *Taking up where her sister had left off.* She deserved everything she had coming to her and a great deal more.

So why couldn't he erase the image of the soft wonder in her eyes when she'd stared up at him in the aftermath of their encounter?

Why couldn't he forget that spontaneous hug?

For a ridiculous, crazy moment he'd been tempted to roll on to his back and hug her in return. Fortunately for both of them, masculine self-preservation had intervened and saved him from an action that would have been as embarrassing as it would have been inexplicable.

The problem, he decided, was that he hadn't expected the sex to be so astonishingly, *spectacularly* good. It had thrown him, as had the unguarded way in which she'd hugged him. He wasn't used to giving or receiving affection. Especially not in the bedroom, where it could be so easily misinterpreted. On the contrary, he was always incredibly careful not to display a fraction more affection than he considered safe and appropriate. He knew better than anyone that women always wanted more from a relationship than men. For him, sex was no more than a physical release. And he intended to keep it that way.

He'd seen firsthand what happened when a man tried to commit to one woman and failed. Hadn't his father spent his entire marriage failing to resist temptation?

The fact that his new bride was astonishingly intelligent and surprisingly good in bed didn't change the fact that he was in this marriage because of her greedy, manipulative streak. And it was a marriage he would never have chosen.

He had no reason to feel guilty.

The marriage had been her choice.

Who could blame him for taking advantage of the situation?

CHAPTER EIGHT

ANGIE woke to find herself alone in the huge bed and she knew instinctively that it was late. Sun poured into the room through the open French windows and the sight of the perfect blue sky should have been sufficient to tempt even the lethargic on to the balcony.

But she didn't move. For a moment she lay there, stunned and disbelieving as her mind trailed over the events of the previous night.

Her body ached in unfamiliar places and her mind was tormented by thoughts that she could neither control nor understand.

What had she done?

She'd slept with the man who had broken her sister's heart. *The man her sister had loved so deeply and planned to marry.*

Horrified by her behaviour, she sat up quickly and covered her face with her hands. She felt *so* ashamed. What on earth had happened to her? She should have pushed him away. She should have refused. *She shouldn't have responded to him.*

Her brain was so full of things that she should and shouldn't have done, she could hardly breathe.

What happened now? What should she do?

She heard a tap on the door and her hands fell from her face as she instinctively pulled the sheet under her chin to cover her nakedness. A woman entered, carrying a tray and followed by several other members of staff.

'Mr Kyriacou gave instructions for your luggage to be brought up. He thought you might like to take breakfast while we unpack your things.'

Things? What things? She'd thought no further than the wedding and she didn't have any luggage.

But cases and boxes started appearing in the room and were then transferred into the adjoining dressing room to be sorted.

The woman smiled. 'I'm Maria, Mr Kyriacou's house-keeper. If you need anything at all, please let me know.'

She melted out of the room and Angie slid out of the bed and hurried to the bathroom, anxious to be dressed by the time Nikos returned. She showered quickly, wrapped herself in a robe that she found neatly folded next to the bath and walked into the dressing room, which was now fully stocked with clothes and shoes.

'You're awake.'

The sound of Nikos's hard tones from behind her made her turn and she instinctively clutched the edges of her robe together. Why, she wondered, did he always look so cool and confident, no matter what the situation? After everything that had happened between them during the night, she felt incredibly shy and self-conscious but he barely cast a glance in her direction.

'Get dressed and meet me downstairs on the terrace.'

She waved a hand at the dressing room. 'I didn't ask for clothes.'

'Consider it one of the perks of being married to me,' he drawled, his voice faintly contemptuous. 'You may be an archaeologist by profession but I'd rather you didn't walk around looking like something that's been unearthed from the dust of Pompeii. If we want to convince everyone that this marriage is real then you at least have to look like a woman that I'm likely to be interested in.'

Insecurity stabbed through her. Last night, for a short blissful time, she'd felt beautiful. He'd *made* her feel beautiful. But clearly everything he'd said had been insincere and why that knowledge should hurt so deeply she didn't understand.

Why should it matter to her that he found her unattractive? Why should she care that being with her clearly embarrassed him?

'No one in their right mind would believe this marriage to be real,' she said stiffly, 'because I would never be interested in a man as shallow as you. And I'm not interested in dressing up and turning myself into the sort of woman who would interest you.'

'You could spend a month with a stylist and never come close. Make an effort,' he advised silkily, 'or I'll drag you back up here and dress you myself. And, before you even contemplate having a tantrum, let me remind you that you were the one who wanted this marriage. Well, now you have what you want and I don't want anyone asking awkward questions. I don't want anything to attract the attention of the media. I don't want the paparazzi snapping you with a sulky expression on your face and then wondering why. When you leave the villa you're the blushing bride on her honeymoon. Remember that.' Without giving her a chance to reply, he strode out of the room, leaving her close to tears.

Why did he care so much about his public image? Why didn't he just not buy newspapers if the contents bothered him so much? She didn't understand him at all. They were *so* different.

Whatever had possessed her to demand that he marry her? *Just whom exactly had she believed she'd be punishing?*

The truth was, she hadn't thought at all. Feeling miserable

and unsettled, she rifled through the rails. If she had stopped to think, then she never would have suggested such a thing. She wasn't the sort of woman who could ever be comfortable with a man like Nikos. He was accustomed to women who cultivated a level of glamour that she couldn't begin to match. Being with him just brought out all her age old insecurities and threatened a degree of social exposure that she'd been avoiding all her adult life.

She stared at the clothes, unsure what to select, her mother's voice echoing in her head. *You haven't a clue how to dress, Angelina. You're so dowdy. You're so frumpy. You're nothing like your sister.* Her hand closed over a simple white top and a pair of loose turquoise trousers. She knew she was nothing like her sister. Tiffany had been truly beautiful and extremely confident. Holding the trousers against the shoe rack, she selected a pair of strappy sandals that looked about the same colour. Was she supposed to wear the same colour or a different colour? Suddenly she wished she had someone she could ask. *Tiffany would have known the answer.*

Wondering how he could have known her size, Angie didn't even glance in the mirror because her confidence was already at rock-bottom and she didn't need visual evidence of her physical deficiencies to push it down any further.

Nikos had made four phone calls in rapid succession and finished his coffee by the time Angelina walked hesitantly on to the terrace.

The first thing he noticed was that she'd left her hair loose. The second was that she looked incredible in the clothes that had been selected for her.

The simple white top moulded discreetly to her body, hinting at tempting curves underneath, and the well-cut trousers skimmed her long legs—*legs that he'd felt wrapped around him the night before as he'd thrust into her welcoming heat.*

Lust thudded through him and he gave a soft curse and reminded himself that a decent set of clothes and a surprising talent between the sheets didn't change the person she was. She, her sister and her mother all shared the same genes.

And, if it weren't for the urgent necessity of restoring the diamond to his family with the minimum of fuss, he never would have agreed to her ridiculous terms.

She was wearing no make-up, her face was pale and she looked vulnerable and uncertain as she walked to the table and sat down.

For some reason that he couldn't identify, the vulnerability increased his irritation by several degrees and suddenly he wished she'd glare at him or issue one of her dignified retorts.

Instead she sat in silence, her eyes bruised from lack of sleep, her lips still slightly swollen from the ravages of the night.

One of his staff stepped forward and poured her coffee.

'Thank you.' Her husky voice curled itself around his senses and suddenly he contemplated cancelling the business meeting so that he could take her straight back to bed and spend the day furthering her sexual education.

Shocked by the strength of the urge to grab her and drag her across the table towards him, he rose to his feet in a forceful movement, almost knocking the chair over. 'I'll see you later.'

She looked up. 'You're leaving? Already? You haven't finished your coffee.'

The fact that she found his behaviour surprising simply increased his irritation. 'I'm not in the habit of explaining my movements to anyone, least of all a wife with tendencies towards blackmail,' he informed her in a deadly tone. 'I have work to do.'

He could easily have worked from his state-of-the-art office in the villa but had decided that it would be better to work from his office in Athens. It was the only way he could be sure that he wouldn't be tempted to leave his desk and seek out his new wife for another hasty round of mindless sex.

Her fingers played nervously with the coffee cup and her blue eyes slid away from his. 'When will you be back?'

'When I want to be.' Nikos reached forward and picked up his phone from the table, noting the flush in her cheeks with a certain grim satisfaction.

At this present moment in time he'd be hard pressed to know which one of them was finding this marriage the worst punishment.

'And what am I supposed to do while you're gone?'

He slipped the phone into his pocket and gave a casual shrug. 'The way you choose to entertain yourself in my absence is of absolutely no interest to me. This is Crete. I'm sure you'll find some mud to dig in, if you look hard enough. It shouldn't be a problem for you, given that your family seem to specialise in dirty tactics.'

Her narrow shoulders stiffened. 'I'm trying to be civil and you refuse even to meet me halfway.'

'I don't require you to be civil. I have no interest in your personality at all. I just require you to strip naked and lie in my bed whenever I demand it,' he said softly, watching as the flush deepened. 'That, *agape mou*, is what I expect from our marriage and from you. You chose this marriage and you made the rules.'

'I didn't think you meant—'

'Clearly there are no end of things that you didn't think through,' he informed her in a helpful tone. 'If it's any consolation, that lack of attention to detail is surprisingly common, even amongst experienced businessmen. It's why I always win. You see, I *do* think things through.'

He reached for his jacket and she leaned across the table and caught his arm. 'Wait. Before you go, there's something I need to ask you.'

The touch of her slender fingers send a stab of lust through his body and the intensity of his reaction stoked his anger still further. 'My pilot is waiting.'

'Was it here?' Her voice was small. 'I need to know whether it was here that my sister died.'

He hesitated and then moved his arm, watching as her hand dropped to her side. 'You sister was in my villa in Athens when she fell. I never brought her here.' Memories stirred inside him and his mouth tightened. How, he wondered to himself as he strode towards the helicopter pad, had he ended up in a situation that he'd been careful to avoid all his life?

His expression grim, he was forced to admit that he hadn't thought things through either. At the time he'd needed the jewel and had been determined to turn her 'punishment' right back at her. But at the moment, he thought to himself with a complete lack of humour, it would be difficult to identify exactly who was suffering the worse punishment.

She didn't understand why he was so mad.

Surely she was the one who should be angry, given that it was her sister who had been in love with him? Her sister he'd left broken-hearted.

But he was behaving as though she'd been totally unreasonable. Maybe she had overreacted a little, she conceded, wishing now that she'd tried to view the situation calmly, but even he should surely be able to admit that he'd behaved extremely badly.

And having to think about the way he treated people wouldn't do him any harm, she told herself firmly.

Obviously he just *hated* having to pay for his crimes. His normal pattern was to sleep with a woman and move on.

Which meant that her punishment was working, didn't it? She wanted him to think twice before he hurt another woman. And now he was stuck with her. And, judging from the black look on his handsome face, her plan was succeeding beyond expectation.

Clearly last night hadn't been anything special for him. Far from it. He hadn't exactly lingered in the bed, waiting for more, had he?

Exhausted from lack of sleep and endless sex, miserably self-conscious and feeling totally out of place, Angie sipped her coffee and wondered how she was going to spend her day.

She heard the helicopter take off and stared up into the perfect blue sky, watching as it lifted and then sped across the sea. Where was he going?

Anywhere, she thought dully, as long as it wasn't near her.

Which was a good thing. Absolutely. It would be a blessing to be relieved of his ice-cold, sarcastic line in conversation.

In the end she spent the day quietly, exploring the grounds of his beautiful villa, sitting on the beach and swimming in his fabulous pool, which just appeared to drop straight into the ocean.

If it hadn't been for a constant nervous awareness that Nikos would eventually arrive home and end her idyll, she could have believed that she'd been dropped straight into the middle of paradise. Except that the paradise was dulled by the knowledge that she'd spent the night with the man that her sister had loved.

She wandered down the steps that led to the private beach, deep in thought. How had it happened? *How had her desire to teach him a lesson turned into a lesson of her own?* A faint ripple of sexual awareness, an echo of the night before, passed through her body, a reminder of the part of herself that he'd awakened. Disturbed by the feeling, she sat down on the warm sand, staring at the perfect curve of the bay.

'You opened the box, Pandora,' she whispered in a hoarse voice as she curled her toes into the sand and hugged her knees with her arms. 'You've released something that you'll never again be able to lock away. It's going to be with you for ever.'

Because now she knew what she was capable of feeling.

But, even knowing that, she wasn't going to let him touch her again. Last night had been a mistake and everyone made mistakes. The important thing was not to repeat them.

She sat for ages, just watching the sea, and then finally wandered back upstairs to the bedroom. It was late in the afternoon and she took another shower and was standing in the bedroom wondering what to wear when she heard the helicopter arrive.

She froze, her heart pounding against her chest, and moments later Nikos strolled into the bedroom.

'Already naked and waiting for me,' he drawled with sardonic humour as he dropped a black case on to the floor. 'You're learning fast, I'll say that for you.'

Clutching the towel, she started to back away from him but she couldn't drag her eyes from his face. *He was unbelievably handsome.* 'I was just about to dress.'

'Don't waste your time.' Without further preamble, he slid an arm round her waist and pulled her hard against him, leaving her in no doubt as to his intentions. 'I thought about you today—'

Disturbed by her dreamy contemplation of his thick, dark lashes, she tried to concentrate. 'Y-you did?'

'Unfortunately, yes.' His dark brows were locked in an ominous frown as his mouth hovered above hers. 'I was planning your next lesson.'

'Lesson?' She could feel the warmth of his breath against her mouth and her lips parted in invitation. 'Lesson in what?'

'Sexual relations. I think you're ready to move on to the intermediate level,' he murmured, lowering his mouth to hers and delivering a lingering kiss. 'Last night was the beginner's course. You passed with honours, by the way, Dr Kyriacou. Obviously that brain of yours makes you a fast learner.'

She knew she ought to lift a hand and slap his arrogant face but already her pelvis throbbed and the now familiar feeling of heat was starting to spread through her limbs. Instead of hitting him, her hands slid up the front of his shirt and quickly released the buttons, revealing a tantalising expanse of male chest. She forgot her promise to herself not to let him touch her again. *Forgot that her sister had loved this man.* In fact she forgot everything except the tempting feel of his smooth skin under her seeking fingers. She slid her hands up his chest and hooked them round his neck and he brought his head down and kissed her hard, the thrust of his tongue a merciless, passionate invasion that bordered on the angry. His hand cupped her bottom through the towel and then she felt him give an impatient tug and felt cool air slide over her skin as the damp towel slipped to the floor.

His mouth still on hers, both his hands slid to her bottom and held her hard against him and then he moved slightly and she gave a little gasp as she felt his fingers touching her intimately.

'I want you again. I've been thinking about this all day,' he groaned as he dipped his fingers inside, causing her to gasp and tighten her grip on his neck.

She ought to resist him. She *knew* she ought to resist him, but she couldn't.

'Stop doing that,' she begged against his mouth but he just gave a low laugh and backed her towards the bed, the hard thrust of his arousal pressing against her naked flesh.

'Why stop something so good?' He slid his hands up her body and took her arms firmly in his, removing them from his neck, placing them instead on the waistband of his trousers. His eyes glittered dark and dangerous, issuing a direct challenge, and she felt her heart pound against her chest.

Every part of her body throbbed with an urgency that she couldn't fight. Her fingers struggled with the clasp of his trousers and then the zip until she felt the silken hardness of his erection brush against her fingers.

His breathing harsh and unsteady, he muttered something in Greek and then turned her so that she was facing the bed.

Confused, she was just about to ask what he was intending to do, when he piled several pillows in front of her and pushed her over them.

Suddenly feeling intensely vulnerable, aware that her bottom was facing him, she tried to straighten but she felt the warm, moist flick of his tongue trailing down between her thighs and she gave a strangled cry of disbelief and clutched at the pillows, her hair falling forward, her eyes tightly closed.

Sensation exploded around her as his tongue explored every detail of her womanhood and she was just about to beg him to stop, when she felt his strong fingers digging into her soft flesh as he took her bottom in his hands to hold her steady. She felt the blunt tip of his erection teasing her gently and then he entered her in a series of purposeful thrusts that sent her soaring into an orgasm so explosive that she bit down on the pillow rather than risk allowing the cries to leave her throat.

He didn't slow his thrusts, his rhythm dominating and primitive in its force, the only sound in the room the harshness of his breathing and the slick sound of bare flesh against bare flesh.

She heard him groan something in Greek and then felt his

hands tighten on her hips as he ground deep, emptying himself into her.

He withdrew, lifted her limp compliant body and turned her to face him, his breathing still unsteady. He stroked a hand through her tangled hair and studied her flushed cheeks.

'Lesson number two, passed with honours.'

Then he released her so suddenly that she plopped down on to the bed.

It was only when he stepped out of his trousers and strolled towards the shower that she realised that he hadn't even bothered undressing.

So much for her resolution about resisting him.

The moment he came within touching distance she just couldn't keep her hands off him and she didn't understand it. She didn't understand what happened to her when he touched her. Logic would say that she would never be able to respond to this man. They had *nothing* in common and he'd broken her sister's heart. On top of that, there was no affection or warmth in his lovemaking and she couldn't pretend that there was. It was a basic, carnal sexual experience with no emotional connection at all, certainly not on his part. If anything, he seemed angry with her again, just as he'd seemed angry this morning after the night they'd shared.

And she was angry with him too, she reminded herself with something close to desperation.

This man had led her sister on. Had promised marriage.

And yet, when he walked into the room, her stomach flipped. And when he touched her she was lost. When he touched her, her brain emptied and she cared about nothing except her body and what he could make her feel.

It was wrong.

So *wrong*. And she didn't understand it.

She was so deep in thought that she didn't hear the sound

of the shower being turned off, didn't realise that he'd finished until she glanced up and saw him standing in front of her, doing up the buttons of a white dress shirt.

'You have ten minutes to dress,' he said in a cool voice as he reached for a black bow-tie. 'We're going out.'

'Out?' Hideously self-conscious, she bent and retrieved the towel from the floor, holding it in front of herself. 'Out where?'

'To a charity ball.' He snapped out the words, his fingers swift and sure as he secured the tie. 'Boring, but there you are.'

A charity ball? She felt a twinge of horror and shrank back on the bed. 'No, don't make me do that. I really don't want to go.'

'It isn't optional.'

He was angry about something. Really angry. 'Please.' Her voice cracked slightly and she hated herself for betraying just how anxious social events made her. 'I'm hopeless at that sort of thing. I never know what to wear or what to say. I'm hopeless at mindless chit chat. I'll just show you up, embarrass you—'

He pulled on his trousers and reached for his jacket. 'I need a partner and, thanks to you, I have no choice about who I go with. Get dressed. If you're worried that you'll say the wrong thing, just don't open your mouth.'

'Who will they think I am?'

'My wife.' He gave a mocking smile. 'You'll be the object of no end of speculation. They'll all be guessing as to why you were the one to finally hook me.'

Which meant that everyone would be staring at her. And gossiping. Shrinking inside, Angie closed her eyes and shook her head. 'I'm not getting dressed.'

'Fine, then you go naked, which should guarantee that you'll be the centre of attention.' He reached out and pulled her to her feet and suddenly her mouth was within a breath of his. Her heart thundered out of control and he gave a faint smile of understanding. 'Not now, *agape mou*. Unfortunately we don't have time. But later, definitely. That's a promise. Now, get dressed.'

Wondering why he could have this effect on her when she couldn't stand him, hating herself for not being able to control the reaction of her body, she stumbled into the dressing room and stared at the racks of clothes.

She felt woefully inadequate and out of her depth and she turned to him. 'Please—' her voice was hoarse '—tell me what I should wear.'

His eyes met hers and for a moment she braced herself for a sarcastic comment. Braced herself to be left to her own devices.

But then he muttered something in Greek under his breath and strode towards the rail, reaching for a dress. 'Wear this. It will suit you. Choosing shoes is beyond me but anything with a high heel will do.'

She was so pathetically grateful for his help that she almost hugged him. Then she reminded herself that he was cold and heartless and was probably only helping her because he didn't want her to embarrass him by wearing something unsuitable.

She wriggled into the green silk dress, pulling a face as she saw the plunging neckline.

'This is too low—' She made a movement to tug it upwards but he reached out to stop her.

'Wear it. You have an amazing body. It's a crime to hide it under shapeless navy trousers and an ill-fitting jacket.'

An amazing body?

Flushed with embarrassment and *hating* him for teasing her, she dragged the dress away from him, feeling the hot sting of tears behind her eyes. 'It's really cruel of you to tease me about my body. You have no respect for my feelings.'

He gave her a curious look. 'You really do have a low opinion of yourself, don't you?'

She flushed, thoroughly confused. Could his comment have been genuine? No, of course it couldn't. She *knew* she didn't have an amazing body.

An hour later she sat in a state of self-conscious misery, staring at the elaborate confection on her plate, aware that everyone was glancing at her and talking. Speculating.

She sat in silence at the dinner table, picking at her food and wondering why, if sex was a stress reliever, Nikos always seemed even more irritable after he'd made love to her.

Not 'made love', she corrected herself hastily. There was nothing loving or romantic about what they shared. It was everything desperate and dirty.

She blushed slightly and put down her fork, incredibly uncomfortable with the sudden image of herself that flared in her mind—*bent over the bed with him thrusting hard inside her in an almost animal-like possession.*

By her side, Nikos was conversing about foreign investments in rapid Greek and she suddenly felt desperately sorry for the man seated on her left. He'd probably anticipated an evening with a society beauty and instead he'd been placed next to her. A silent companion with nothing to offer. Her confidence at rock-bottom, she struggled for something bland and uncontroversial to say.

Perhaps reading her mind, he turned towards her, his expression stiff. 'You are English? I'm afraid my English is not good.'

'I'm sure your English is excellent but I'm very happy to speak Greek,' she assured him hastily in that language, hugely grateful that he'd made the effort to speak to her at all. Seeing the flash of surprise and pleasure in his eyes she relaxed slightly, relieved to have at least *something* to recommend her. 'Do you work for Nikos?'

The man gave a wry smile. 'Although most of western civilisation seems to work for your husband, Mrs Kyriacou, I am not one of them.' He reached for his wineglass. 'I'm Dimitri Vassaras and I work for the government in the Department of Culture and Science. I am responsible for maintaining our heritage. One of our major projects at the moment is exploring ways of protecting archaeological sites from looters. All very boring for a pretty lady like you.'

'On the contrary.' Forgetting her worries about not fitting in, Angie leaned forward, her face animated as she responded in fluent Greek. 'It's a subject that interests me greatly. The threat of looting often means that artefacts are removed quickly without recording their proper context and that means that precious information is lost—' Aware that he was staring at her in stunned amazement, she coloured and stopped speaking.

He cleared his throat. 'You are interested in archaeology?'

Remembering too late that Nikos had advised her to stay quiet and not talk, Angie was about to respond in a suitably vague way when Nikos spoke.

'My wife has sufficient qualifications to meet even your exacting standards, Dimitri,' he drawled, his eyes fixed on Angie's face. 'And her knowledge of our language is an added bonus.'

Realising that she had now revealed that she spoke his language, she tried to read his expression and failed. Was he angry? Irritated? As usual, those thick, dark lashes half shielded his eyes, giving nothing away.

He was *so* difficult to read.

'I am truly honoured,' Dimitri said, taking her hand and lifting it to his lips, 'to have the opportunity to speak to someone who has a real understanding of our treasures.'

'The preservation of archaeological finds is a really important issue,' Angie said quietly, flushing slightly under Dimitri's approving gaze. 'We go to great lengths to carefully record information as we excavate a site layer by layer. Anything that disturbs that process jeopardises the quality of the information.'

'You must really approve of your husband's approach, then,' Dimitri said warmly as he reached for his wine. 'I know of few other men of his standing who would acknowledge the potential archaeological significance of a site and willingly sacrifice commercial opportunity in favour of the preservation of our natural heritage.'

'Not willingly, Dimitri,' Nikos said dryly, lifting his glass to his lips. 'I complained a great deal, if you remember. You just didn't listen to me.'

'You complained only until we pointed out the enormous relevance of the site,' Dimitri responded, turning to Angie with enthusiasm. 'We are about to start a major archaeological survey and excavation project which we think will reveal evidence of early Bronze Age civilization—'

'Dimitri,' Nikos interrupted him, 'if you're about to deliver a lecture then you need to remember that tonight is all about funding and I'm never at my most generous when I'm bored.'

'I no longer have any concerns about the funding of this project,' Dimitri said happily and Nikos raised an eyebrow, his voice a sardonic drawl.

'You don't?'

'Why would I need to convince you of the benefits of investing money in this project when your beautiful, talented wife can do that for me?' Dimitri beamed. 'With your permission I shall outline the details of the project and Mrs Kyriacou can use her special relationship with you to influence your donation.'

'Is that right?' Nikos turned to Angie, his eyes resting on her face in brooding contemplation. 'Are you going to use your special relationship with me, *agape mou*?'

Confused by his soft tone and by the mockery she saw in

his gaze, she coloured slightly and turned to Dimitri, determined not to allow Nikos to undermine her confidence. She was going to use whatever means at her disposal to get through the evening and the fact that she possessed certain knowledge was merely to her advantage. 'I'd love to hear more about the project.'

Others on the table were drawn into the discussion and she soon realised that she was actually seated with some of the top people in the Greek government. Soon they were all conversing in Greek, discussing the problems of obtaining research grants and the search for additional sponsorship.

'That's where I come in,' Nikos drawled, shifting slightly so that a waiter could remove his plate. 'I'm the sponsorship.'

'Sponsorship is integral to archaeology,' Angie observed quietly and Dimitri smiled.

'Your husband would have us believe that he does nothing more than throw money in our direction while remaining in ignorance and yet we all know that his knowledge surpasses that of many respected archaeologists.'

Angie hid her surprise. Did she know that? No, she didn't. The man she knew was only interested in sex and money. Wondering if they were talking about the same person, Angie looked at Dimitri in disbelief and then turned her gaze to Nikos, who was subjecting her to a cool appraisal.

'Believe it or not, my wife and I haven't yet spent much time talking about early Minoan artefacts,' he said softly and Dimitri gave an indulgent smile.

'Well, of course you haven't. You're newly married. But what a partnership!' His face glowed with excitement as he glanced round the table at the others. 'Dr Kyriacou will be able to bring a great deal to our latest project. Nikos, now we don't just want your money, we want your wife!'

'I had no idea she would prove so popular.'

Dimitri smiled, either ignoring or failing to notice the slightly dangerous edge to his tone.

'Tell me, Dr Kyriacou, have you had a proper tour of Knossos yet? It is Crete's most famous ancient site.'

'I visited it a few years ago,' Angie replied, her eyes on Nikos's profile. There was something about the stillness of his body that troubled her. 'Not recently. I'm looking forward to another visit.'

'Then I would be honoured to be your guide,' Dimitri said immediately and Nikos rose to his feet, his hand round Angie's wrist.

'Unfortunately I've already arranged to take Angelina there myself,' he said smoothly, the pressure of his hand on her arm forcing her to rise as well. 'Now, if you'll excuse me, I'm going to dance with my wife.'

Her cheeks flushed, aware of the indulgent smiles of those watching, Angie almost stumbled as she tried to keep up with him in the unfamiliar high heels. 'I can't even walk in these things, let alone dance,' she muttered and his fingers tightened on her wrist and he swung her into his arms as they reached the centre of the dance floor.

Aware of the strong athletic length of his body against hers, Angie felt her body start to quiver and melt in anticipation and when he slid a leisurely hand down her back and anchored her hard against him she gave a soft gasp.

'Flirt with Dimitri again,' he warned in a deadly tone, 'and he'll be lying dead at the bottom of one of his excavations along with bones and bits of pottery.'

'Flirt?' Wishing she wasn't so conscious of every throbbing masculine inch of him, she placed a hand on his chest in an attempt to push him away slightly. 'I didn't flirt.'

'He couldn't take his eyes off you. I've known Dimitri for

almost ten years and I've never seen him so animated. Clearly he's very turned on by all those letters after your name.'

She couldn't think straight while he was this close. 'I don't understand why you would even care. It's ridiculous to be so possessive when you have no interest in me yourself.' She tried to pull away but he held her fast, moving her round the dance floor with a smooth confidence that was the only thing that prevented her from stumbling in the unfamiliar high heels.

'What I think of you is irrelevant. You're my wife. Just don't think about accepting any invitations he might offer.'

Confused and infuriated by the feelings that were scorching her body, she was suddenly determined to challenge his slightly predatory treatment of her. 'I'll accept any invitation I like if they're interesting. The terms of our pre-nuptial agreement don't prevent me being seen with another man.'

'But *I* would prevent it,' Nikos informed her with lethal emphasis, slipping a hand under her chin and forcing her to look at him. His eyes glittered dark and dangerous. 'If you're fantasising about Dimitri, then I should warn you that he has a young wife and child waiting for him back in Athens. Or perhaps that wouldn't stop you.'

His slightly contemptuous tone made her frown slightly. Why would he think, or even care if she was fantasising about Dimitri? And why would he believe that the fact that Dimitri was married wouldn't stop her?

'You make me sound like some sort of sexual tease and yet we both know I'm nothing like that.'

He stared down at her for a long moment and she had the distinct feeling that he wanted to say something more but he didn't so she spoke again, suddenly needing to bridge the ominous silence.

'He's an interesting, w-well-educated man,' she stammered quietly, wondering why such a bland, innocuous observation could make his expression darken still further. 'Any interest I have in him would be purely academic. If I spent time with him it would just be to exchange views and learn from each other.'

'The only learning you're going to do is from me,' he growled, tightening his grip on her waist and propelling her from the dance floor towards the exit.

'We can't leave without saying goodbye—'

'I'm the guest of honour. I can do anything I like. No one is interested in my manners, only my wallet.' He deposited her in the passenger seat of his low, deadly-looking Ferrari and slid into the seat next to her, his strong hands confident on the wheel as he drove out of town back towards the villa.

'This is so embarrassing!' Angie glanced back over her shoulder towards the museum. 'I should have said goodbye. They'll be offended.'

'The only thing that will offend them is if I refuse the funding they're begging for.'

'Holding the purse-strings doesn't give you the right to be rude,' she said stiffly, turning her head to look out of the window. The sight of his arrogant, handsome profile made her entire body weak with longing and she hated herself for feeling that way about a man as basic and primitive as Nikos. He was different from every man she'd ever met before. His forceful, controlling personality should have been completely repellent to her. 'I thought Dimitri was charming and had lovely manners.'

Her rash, impulsive remark was greeted by ominous silence and when she risked a glance towards Nikos she clashed with night-black eyes and her stomach performed a series of alarming acrobatics. A powerful awareness flared between them. They shouldn't have been right together and yet there was an electrifying connection. *A connection that defied logic and scorned convention.*

He dragged his gaze back to the road and she closed her eyes briefly, reminding herself to breathe.

Was it just her?

Was it just her who felt like this? And then she saw that his hands were tight on the wheel as he coaxed the car round the tight bends of the road and knew that he was feeling it too.

Without warning, he swung the car to the left down a rough track and she gave a soft gasp of shock and clutched at the seat. 'Shouldn't you slow down a bit?'

'I don't feel like slowing down.' He stopped the car and suddenly she was aware of the warm night air and the soft murmur of the sea.

'This isn't your villa. Where are we?'

'Somewhere we won't be disturbed.' He yanked open her door and closed his hand around her wrist so that she was given no choice but to climb out of the car.

'You're behaving very oddly, if you don't mind me saying,' she muttered and then stumbled as she discovered the impossibility of walking on the sand in high heels.

Without speaking, he scooped her into his arms and carried her to the water's edge and then slipped both shoes from her feet before lowering her to the ground.

She felt the damp sand beneath her bare feet and then nothing but the hot, demanding press of his mouth against hers, the erotic lick of his tongue and the tempting throb of his male body. 'Nikos—' Stunned by the sudden assault on her senses, she sank against him and felt his hands, sure and confident, sliding the dress down her trembling, compliant body. 'You can't do that; it will be ruined,' she groaned against his mouth but it was too late because the dress had slipped to the sand and she felt the warm night air glide over her bare skin.

'I'll buy you another one.' Still kissing her, he stripped off his jacket, hooked a leg behind hers, gently knocked her off balance and lay her down, his body hard on hers. 'I want you and I want you right now,' he muttered in Greek and she made a sound somewhere between laughter and desperation. *He wanted her.* Why did those words send a tremor of exultation running through her?

'I want you too.' Her softly spoken Greek ended in a gasp as he closed his mouth round the vulnerable peak of her breast, drawing her inside and teasing her nipple with his tongue. The sudden explosion of excitement was so intense that she shifted her hips in an attempt to ease the frantic ache in her pelvis but his superior weight held her still, allowing her no relief from the delicious torture.

'I know you want me. You just can't help yourself and it's the most incredible turn-on.'

Dizzy with excitement, she felt his fingers slide between her thighs and gave a whimper of desperation. He knew exactly where to touch her, exactly how to touch her, and his skilled assault had her shaking and squirming against his hand. 'Please, Nikos—'

He lifted his head from her breast, his breathing unsteady. In the moonlight it was just possible to make out his features but somehow the semi-darkness just made the encounter all the more erotic. Without speaking, he moved away from her just enough to deal with his trousers and then he lifted her hips and sank inside her with an almost desperate urgency that brought a cry of surprise and relief to her lips.

She felt the velvety thickness of his arousal, the demanding pressure of masculine thrust and wrapped her legs around him, taking him deeper still into her quivering, willing flesh. She was no more capable of resisting the demands of his body than she was her own. And her demands were great. Driven by a primitive urge that she didn't even recognise, she lifted her hips and moved her body to match the rhythm of his. Her nails dug into the hard muscle of his back, her teeth sank into the sleek skin of his shoulder and he acknowledged her need with an increase in his own demands. Drowning in a torrent of sensation, the sudden explosion of her orgasm came without warning and she heard him mutter something in Greek as her body pulsed around his, dragging him from a point of control to sexual oblivion in one single heartbeat.

The night was still warm, the damp sand hard under her back, and she lay with her eyes closed, trying to recover, aware of the throbbing heat of his body inside hers, the soft swish of the sea in the background.

Gradually reality intruded on fantasy and she felt a rush of mortification. 'Oh, my goodness, are we allowed to do this on a beach?'

It was a moment before he replied, but finally he lifted his head and rolled away from her, springing to his feet in a lithe movement that said a great deal about his strength and power given the quantity of energy he'd just expended. 'This is a private beach.' He reached down and pulled her to her feet. 'I own it.'

Well, of course he owned it, she thought wearily. It appeared that he owned everything the eye could see as well as a considerable amount that it couldn't.

Horribly aware that, once again, she was naked while he was dressed, she stooped to pick up the green silk but he was ahead of her, his hands sure and confident as he slid the fabric over her head and settled it on her curves.

Suddenly she wished he'd say something. Anything.

After what they'd just shared, surely he wanted to say *something*.

But he simply picked up his jacket and her shoes, took her by the hand and led her back to the car.

CHAPTER NINE

NIKOS stood staring at the famous dolphin fresco, wondering what on earth he was doing.

Had he finally lost his grip on sanity?

He had a mountain of work that required his immediate attention, a senior executive team fighting for his time, and yet he'd elected to take the day off to show his new wife around the palace of Knossos.

If that had been his only questionable action then he could perhaps have justified it by telling himself that, since they were married, it was worth investing a little time into the relationship in order to make his life run smoothly.

But the justification lost credibility when he forced himself to confront the fact that the past week had been full of questionable actions.

Each day he'd found himself unable to concentrate in the office and had returned home early with the sole purpose of taking his new wife to bed and trying to work whatever it was that so fascinated him about her out of his system. His lack of success in that direction had been more than demonstrated by his behaviour on the way home from the ball a week ago.

He cursed softly and ran a hand over the back of his neck. His need for her had been so great that he hadn't even been able to wait until they'd arrived home. He'd been so incensed by her praise of Dimitri that he'd pulled the car off the road and taken her on the beach without thought about their surroundings. His single objective had been to drive thoughts of other men out of her head.

And then he laughed. Why was he fooling himself?

The chemistry between them was positively electric. Despite the fact that she was as far from his usual choice of woman that it was possible to be, he found her strangely addictive.

'It's fascinating, isn't it? It has four wings arranged around a central court which is the nucleus of the whole complex.' Her blue eyes bright with excitement and enthusiasm, she stepped up next to him, her fiery hair tucked under a wide-brimmed hat. As usual she was wearing trousers and a simple top and he smiled at the irony of the situation. He'd been involved with plenty of women whose sole idea of fun was exercising his credit card in a designer boutique and then changing outfits on almost an hourly basis.

'Nikos?' She tilted her head and smiled up at him, her blue eyes sparkling. 'Don't you find it fascinating?'

He found *her* fascinating. She was unlike anyone he'd ever met before and he was more and more confused and irritated by his reaction to her. He was used to his relationships being entirely straightforward. He made the rules and women stuck to them. 'You're a very atypical woman.'

Her smile faltered. 'What do you mean by that?'

'I mean that I give you the entire contents of an expensive boutique and you choose to wear virtually the same thing every day. Trousers and a top.'

She blushed and looked down at herself, insecurity showing in that glance. 'I—the clothes are lovely. Thank you. I suppose I'm just not really that good at deciding what should go with what.'

'Why?' He slipped a hand under her chin, forcing her to look at him. 'Why don't you have any confidence in the way you look?'

'Oh—' She gave a faint frown as if it wasn't something she'd considered before. 'Because I know I'm not beautiful. And I'm not great at choosing what to wear. Mum always used to wince when she looked at me. Whatever I wore, she always rolled her eyes and told me I looked wrong—'

'One's family has a great deal to answer for.'

'Does yours?'

Nikos thought of his father and gave a wry smile. 'My family is as dysfunctional as the next.'

'You've never told me anything about your family.'

His hand dropped to his side and he stared down at her, suddenly realising just how close he'd come to sharing intimate details that he'd never shared with anyone. *What was the matter with him?* He *never* talked about his family and if he ever chose to do so it certainly wouldn't be to Tiffany Littlewood's sister.

'There's nothing to tell. But if you're nervous about dressing up, I'll arrange for someone to come and suggest how you might wear the clothes.'

Her eyes widened. 'You'd do that for me?'

'Why not?' He shrugged dismissively. 'It's in my interests to see you wearing something other than trousers. I have a friend in Athens who can help. I'll fly her over and she can spend an afternoon with you.'

'Thank you.' She gave a shy smile. 'I could do with more information on the subject.'

Information. Only Angelina would turn dressing up into something to be studied.

As if to prove where her priorities lay, she suddenly caught his hand and dragged him to see a row of pots, examining them in minute detail.

Her lively interest in her subject was infectious and he took a step back, reminding himself that his sole purpose in being here was to prevent her going with Dimitri.

'This whole area lies on a great seismic site. It's been destroyed by earthquakes on several occasions.' Why should a conversation that was so dull and boring make his nerve-endings hum?

'And been rebuilt—' She grabbed his hand again and pulled him towards a different part of the ruins. 'Come and look at this. You can see how they would have invented the myth of the monster in the Labyrinth, can't you?

She was smiling and he found himself once again noticing the amazing colour of her eyes. When she talked about archaeology or mythology she was a different person, he observed. Confident. Vibrant.

'You don't believe in our Minotaur?'

'A monster, half-man half-bull? I don't think so. But it makes a great story. It was my favourite when I was a child.' She seemed unaware that her hand was still on his arm and he frowned.

'I can imagine you locked in your room, absorbed in a book.'

She blushed slightly and her hand dropped to her side. 'You're not far from the truth. I spent a lot of time in my room or in the library at school. I wasn't a very sociable child. I liked my own company.'

And yet her mother and sister had clearly made socialising a priority. Something jarred in his brain and he reminded himself that, although she was clearly unlike her sister in many obvious ways, she insisted on excusing and approving her sister's behaviour.

'We need to leave.' His tone was rough as he glanced at his watch. 'We have another dinner tonight.'

'Really?' Her face brightened and his insides clenched.

'If you're hoping to renew your acquaintance with Dimitri, then it's only fair to warn you that he won't be there tonight.'

'It will be nice to meet some of your other friends and colleagues.' She bent down to examine a piece of stone more closely. 'Can you see the pattern?'

'I thought you hated socialising?'

'I do usually.' She stood up and brushed her hair out of her eyes. 'But that's because the conversation at these events is usually so superficial and I feel out of place. The ball last week was like spending an evening at the University. They were lovely people.'

Recalling just how many of his previous girlfriends had threatened to walk out of similar events, declaring them boring, Nikos frowned. 'Tonight will be a different set of people. Bankers.'

'Fine.' Her eyes fixed on something behind his shoulder. 'Oh, can we just take a closer look at that?'

Wondering what had happened to the woman who was afraid to dress up and go out, Nikos allowed himself to be led along the dusty path to another section of the Palace.

She couldn't remember when she'd enjoyed a day more. Nikos had been interesting and entertaining company and his depth of knowledge on Minoan art and history had astonished her. And she was more and more confused about him.

'You know such a lot about Knossos.'

'I'm Greek.'

'And that's why?' As they drove back along the coast towards his villa, she sneaked a glance at his profile. What exactly had a man of his obvious intelligence seen in Tiffany? She'd loved her sister but love had never made her blind. She'd known that her sister had no interest in anything more serious than clothes or dressing up. But she'd been truly beautiful. And, according to her mother, that was what mattered to a man like Nikos.

To him women were entertainment, nothing more. When he became bored, he moved on. But why would a man who was famed for avoiding commitment propose marriage to her sister? Why would he have given her sister the Brandizi diamond? None of it made sense.

'You're staring at me.' His smooth observation brought a flush to her cheeks.

'Did you ever love her or was it just about sex?' Her impulsive question was greeted by a tightening of his mouth.

'I refuse to discuss your sister. I thought I'd made that clear.'

'I'm trying to understand you—'

'Don't bother. Being understood is not high on my list of requirements in a partner.' He slowed the car as they approached the villa and he waited for the enormous iron gates to swing open.

'But we're married. We're spending time together.' The powerful car purred along the drive and the gates swung closed behind them.

'We are married because you insisted on it,' he reminded her in a cool tone as he parked the car, 'and we're spending time together because you effectively banned all other women from my life.'

She bit her lip, attacked by insecurities. She'd thought they'd had a nice day. She'd thought that he'd actually enjoyed her company and yet here he was making it clear that he was with her under sufferance and the knowledge made her utterly miserable. Why? Why should she be miserable when she'd achieved exactly what she'd wanted to achieve? She'd wanted to punish him and she had.

Why was she disappointed that the intimacy she'd felt during the day had somehow disappeared?

'We have a dinner to attend tonight,' he reminded her as they walked towards the steps of the villa. 'We'll be leaving in an hour.'

This time she didn't bother arguing or asking questions. Instead she just showered quickly and walked through to select a suitable dress.

Determined to be less hesitant and clueless than usual, she selected what she hoped was a suitable dress and changed.

'I'll say this for you, it's refreshing to be with a woman who doesn't need at least half a day to prepare for an evening out.' He strolled towards her, staggeringly handsome in a dinner jacket, his dark hair still damp from the shower. 'That dress suits you. And I love you in high heels. You have fantastic legs. From now on, trousers are banned.'

Angie blushed and ran a hand over her hips in a self-conscious gesture. The midnight-blue silk fell from tiny straps on her shoulders and skimmed her curves, stopping just short of the knee. It made her feel beautiful and feminine. 'It's pretty,' she said softly, glancing sideways at her reflection in the mirror. 'I actually didn't realise how much I could enjoy dressing up.' The confession surprised her but she suddenly realised that it was true. Tonight, for the first time in her life, it had suddenly felt important to select the right thing to wear.

Why? Why did her appearance suddenly matter?

Her eyes were still on the woman in the mirror. She barely recognised herself. Her eyes and skin glowed with health and the subtle application of make-up made her mouth seem fuller and her eyes seem bigger.

Nikos strolled up behind her and her eyes met his in the mirror. 'Your mother did you a disservice.' His voice was rough. 'You're a very sexy woman.'

The unexpected compliment startled her. 'I—I don't think

so. I'm so used to comparing myself to—' She broke off, not wanting to spoil the moment by mentioning her sister.

'Tiffany.'

'You saw her. She was beautiful. She made men do stupid things.'

His mouth tightened. 'I'm entirely aware of that.'

'Of course you are—' Hating the reminder that he'd been with her sister, she glanced away. 'No man could resist Tiffany.'

'I still don't understand why that affected whether you dressed up or not.'

'I suppose I didn't even bother to compete,' she said quietly. 'From the moment she was born, Tiffany was the pretty one. You should have seen her as a baby. Completely gorgeous. No one ever looked further than her blonde hair. Did you know that she was clever?' She felt tears prick her eyes and blinked them away. 'I wanted her to study and use her brain but she always thought that was a waste of time. She just wanted to fall in love and get married.'

'Preferably to the richest guy possible.'

'And why not?' She turned on him angrily, spirited in her defence of her sister. 'It's so easy for you to judge and yet you know absolutely *nothing* about our lives! Have you any idea how hard it was for her? Dad had one affair after another and spent money until he was bankrupt. One minute he was showering Tiffany with presents and the next he'd died of a heart attack and Mum was moving us out of our very comfortable four-bedroom detached house into a tiny flat with less light than a cave. Can you really blame Tiffany for wanting more?' She broke off and bit her lip, wishing she hadn't revealed so much. *Why had she told him all those things?*

'You believe that the end always justifies the means?'

His question threw her and she frowned. 'No. No, I don't believe that, of course I don't. I'm just saying that you don't have all the facts.'

There was a long silence and a tiny muscle worked in his bronzed cheek. 'No, *agape mou*,' he said softly, 'I think you're the one who doesn't have all the facts. And now we need to leave or we will be late.'

She followed him to the car, the frown still on her face. What did he mean, she didn't have all the facts? Of course she had the facts! She had far more than he did! She'd *known* Tiffany. She'd understood her, even if she hadn't always approved of her slightly wayward behaviour.

She was silent all the way in the car, brooding on his words. Part of her wanted to question him further but held herself back. Their relationship was already so inflammatory and complicated that the last thing they needed was a row about Tiffany just before appearing at a public function.

'Where are we?'

'At the museum,' he drawled, clamping a hand round her wrist and pulling her out of the car. 'Smile. There will be cameras.'

He'd barely finished his sentence before a flash of light blinded her and she gave a tiny gasp of shock.

'Just smile,' Nikos instructed, taking the steps up to the museum at a furious pace and forcing her to follow. 'They're not allowed inside, it's a private function.'

'Where are we going?'

'Fundraising and private view of Crete's antiquities,' he told her, walking through the doors of the museum as if he owned it. 'Right up your street.'

'Why is no one else arriving?'

'I expect they're already here.' He gave a yawn and glanced at his watch. 'We're *extremely* late.'

'We are?' Horrified, she allowed him to lead her into a

large room and then gave a whimper of discomfort as a hush spread over the crowded room and everyone turned to look at them. 'Oh, God—'

'Smile.' Totally relaxed and unconcerned, Nikos hauled her against him and dropped a lingering kiss on her mouth.

Forgetting their audience, her eyes closed, her head spun and it wasn't until he finally lifted his head that she remembered where they were. Embarrassed at drawing even more attention to herself, she stared up at him, her head spinning. 'Why did you do that?'

'To remind them that we're newly married. Now they'll all be convinced we're late because we were having amazing sex.'

'But that's terrible,' she stammered, clutching her bag tightly. 'I don't want them to think that. It isn't true.'

'It would have been true if you hadn't brought up the thorny subject of your sister. I have to confess she has a detrimental effect on my libido.'

'I don't want to talk about my sister.'

'Good, because neither do I.' With a smooth, confident movement he guided her to her chair and introduced her to the people seated at their table.

The names flew in and out of her head and she took a sip of wine for courage, aware that she was once again the object of discussion and speculation.

The talk revolved around the money markets and her mind drifted as she was slowly excluded from the conversation. They spoke Greek, clearly assuming that she wouldn't understand, the interaction between the men so exclusively masculine that her opinions weren't required or sought. Everyone deferred to Nikos, confirming his importance in society and her already firm belief that he was very much the king of the pack. The women on the table exchanged trivial pieces of news, who had been to which social gathering, bought which dress. Unable to join in, Angie sat in silence.

'You're quiet tonight.' By her side, Nikos reached forward and lifted his glass. 'Missing Dimitri?'

His sarcasm stung her. 'He was interesting and very kind to me.'

'Kind?' His dark brows met in a frown. 'How was he kind?'

'He talked to me,' she said simply. 'Made me feel as though I had something to say that mattered.'

His gaze rested on her face for a long moment. 'And these people don't.'

'It's not important.' She flushed and gave a hesitant smile. 'They obviously play an important part in your business. They're all hanging on your every word.'

He looked amused. 'Is that how it seems?'

'Either you're a genuinely wise person or they want something from you,' she said lightly, reaching for her own glass. 'My money is on the latter.'

'You don't have any money,' he reminded her in silky tones, his dark head suddenly disturbingly close to hers, 'but if you want to lay bets, then I can think of a suitable forfeit.'

Her eyes slid to his and her heart thumped hard against her chest. 'They're all wondering why you married me.' And why that should bother her, she didn't understand.

He gave a slow, sexy smile. 'You're wrong, *agape mou*. They have only to look at you to understand why I married you. You look extremely beautiful tonight.'

Her heart sprinted rapidly. She shouldn't care what he thought. His comment shouldn't make her feel good.

Confused, she changed the subject. 'So what do they want from you? Money?'

'Isn't that what everyone wants?' He suppressed a yawn and dropped his napkin on the table.

'Don't you get tired of it? Everyone just fawning over you for money? Don't you ever long to meet someone who isn't afraid to tell you exactly what they think of you?'

'Like you, you mean?' He stood up suddenly and pulled her to her feet. 'Let's go and look round the museum.'

'Are we allowed?'

'Of course. Private view. You should enjoy it. They have some very rare examples of pots here. Right up your street.'

Was there cynicism in his tone? She glanced at his face as they left the room but there was no sign of his usual mockery and he took her on a tour of the museum, again displaying a surprising depth of knowledge about the antiquities.

'Dimitri was right when he said that you know a great deal about archaeology. Did you study it at university?'

He gave a faint smile. 'I read law and then did a business degree. More lucrative.'

'And then you joined your father's business?'

He stilled. 'No. I started my own.'

'Oh—I assumed—'

'My father has different interests.'

She studied his tense profile for a moment, sensing that there was plenty more that he could say on that subject. 'He must be very proud of everything you've achieved.'

Nikos frowned sharply, as if the thought had never occurred to him. 'We never talk about things like that.'

Deciding that he clearly wasn't comfortable with the subject of his family, Angie caught his arm and indicated another pot. 'Look at that. Isn't it amazing?'

'Used for diluting the wine. The ancient Greeks never drank their wine neat. Aren't you glad you didn't live in the Minoan period?'

She grinned. 'If I'd lived in the Minoan period I would have been waiting at your table like a servant. They hadn't exactly heard of equal rights for women.'

'There have been some amazing finds further along the coast—' He outlined an excavation that had taken place a few years earlier and she listened to him, absorbed, and then asked some questions of her own and it was only when she caught sight of a clock that she realised two hours had passed.

'Oh, my goodness—' she lifted a hand to her mouth '—everyone will be wondering where we are. We should go back.'

His gaze lingered on hers. 'What if I don't want to go back?'

Her heart skipped and danced. 'What do they want you to pay for this time?'

'Joint venture. A new hotel complex on the south of the island.' He raised an eyebrow. 'Do I say yes or no?'

'I know nothing about business.'

'But you've already proved yourself to be a fast learner.' His gaze drifted to her mouth and she suddenly found that she couldn't breathe properly.

'I don't think I have the necessary qualifications to advise you.'

'I could teach you.'

As he'd been teaching her so many other things? 'Nikos—'

'Let's go home.' He took her hand in his and led her through the large, echoing halls of the museum and out on to the pavement where his car awaited them.

Two weeks later, Angie lay in bed, drifting in and out of sleep, dimly aware that she was alone in the bed. Nikos had made love to her for most of the night and it had been amazingly, shockingly good. In fact, she found herself wishing that he hadn't been forced to make an early start in order to meet a commitment that he had in Athens. If he hadn't then they might have been making love again at this very moment.

Bemused by her own thoughts, she sat up and tried to shake the sleep from her head.

What had happened to her?

What had happened to the woman who'd had no interest in sex or men?

She no longer recognised herself. There were even moments when she'd started to believe that she was beautiful, thanks in part to the woman who Nikos had flown in from Athens. They'd spent an entire afternoon playing with the contents of Angie's wardrobe and she'd had fun discovering how things could be worn.

And then there was Nikos himself. When he made love to her, she *felt* beautiful. And, far from appearing bored or impatient by her love of antiquities, he actually took the trouble to show her things that he knew would interest her.

And they were talking all the time. About everything. The only subject they avoided was Tiffany.

She rubbed a hand over face, thoroughly confused.

It was becoming harder and harder to remember that he was the man who had hurt her sister. Harder and harder to remember that this marriage wasn't real.

And she was increasingly confused about Nikos. She'd thought him to be a driven male with no interest in anything other than work or sex. But, while it was true that he was driven and naturally controlling, he was also well-educated and possessed a keen mind.

It still confused her that such a man would be interested in Tiffany.

But he did love sex, she reminded herself, sliding out of the bed and padding towards the elegant bathroom. So presumably that was what he'd had in common with her sister.

Wasn't that what her mother was always telling her? That

men weren't interested in conversation. Only in sex and having a good time.

But there was a great deal more to Nikos than a love of sex, as she was beginning to discover.

She ran herself a deep, scented bath and lazed in the water, her mind drifting, and then she dried herself and wandered through to the dressing room, determined to select something really nice to wear in case Nikos arrived home early.

She spent half an hour rifling through the rails, trying various combinations and then finally dressed and stared at herself in the mirror. What exactly had happened to her? Since when had she become obsessed as to whether green suited her better than blue? Since when had she worried about whether the cut of a dress flattered her figure or not?

Since when had she cared whether Nikos thought she looked beautiful or not?

You are a sad, stupid fool, she told herself crossly, slipping her feet into a pair of sandals with impossibly high heels. Two weeks ago she wouldn't have been able to walk in them. But since his comment about liking her legs in high heels she'd found herself trying on the highest heels in her wardrobe and then walking up and down in the privacy of their bedroom until she'd mastered the art.

Which made her no better than the rest of the female population, she thought helplessly as she applied a small amount of make-up to her eyes and streaked a clear gloss over her mouth.

Instead of punishing him, she'd fallen for him.

She stared at her reflection in horror.

She hadn't fallen for him, she told herself quickly. She definitely hadn't. Even if he hadn't been involved with her sister, hadn't contributed at least partly to her death, he was totally wrong for her in every way.

'I'm surprised you're awake.' His deep, dark drawl came

from directly behind her and she turned with a gasp of shock, feeling a rush of pleasure to see him standing there.

She shouldn't be pleased, she reminded herself helplessly. She should be wishing he'd spend longer in the office.

'It's already lunchtime.'

'But you didn't get much rest, did you?' He strolled towards her and brought his mouth down on hers in a kiss that sizzled and reawakened her senses. 'I'm taking you out to lunch.'

She stared at him dizzily. 'Out?'

'If we stay in then I'll just have to take you back to bed,' he drawled softly, taking her hand in his and leading her towards the door. 'And I want to show you the real Crete.'

Shocked by her sudden impulse to tell him that going back to bed would suit her just fine, Angie followed him down the stairs and into the black Ferrari that he'd parked in the drive. 'I thought we'd already seen the real Crete.'

'You've seen historic Crete. Now I want you to see Crete as it is today.'

He drove inland to a tiny taverna hidden amongst olive groves with a stunning view of the mountains and the sea.

Clearly he knew the owners, because he chatted in Greek and then guided her to a table shaded by leaves. A faint breeze whispered across the terrace and she watched as he ordered food and wine, more relaxed and at home than she could ever remember seeing him.

'What is this place?'

He was a man who owned numerous properties and private jets, a man who travelled the world on business and yet he'd chosen to bring her to a tiny restaurant populated by friendly locals.

'Jannis serves the best food on Crete,' he told her, leaning forward to fill her glass from the jug. 'After trying his lamb, you'll never eat anywhere else again.'

His unexpected smile made her breath catch. 'You're home earlier than I expected. Was your meeting successful this morning?'

'Extremely boring.' He sat back as Jannis placed a number of dishes on the table between them. 'Next week I have to attend a meeting in Athens about the project Dimitri told you about. I want you to come. Try these. Dolmades—stuffed vine leaves. Delicious.' He placed the food on her plate and she stared at him.

'Me?'

'Yes, you.' He gave a careless shrug of his broad shoulders and helped himself to food. 'You understand what they're talking about. I want to make sure they spend my money wisely. You can translate all that archaeological waffle.'

She felt a rush of pleasure and then put her fork down, thoroughly confused by her own thoughts and by his unexpected invitation. *This wasn't the way their relationship was supposed to be.*

'You're not eating. You don't like vine leaves?'

'I love it—' She glanced down at her plate. 'It's just that—'

'What?'

'Nothing.' She smiled and picked up her fork again, suddenly reluctant to spoil this special lunch by delving too deeply into what was going on in their relationship. 'Tell me how you met Jannis.'

They sat in the taverna, ate, drank and talked until late afternoon and finally Nikos rose to his feet and wandered into the kitchen to settle the bill and say goodbye to Jannis.

The older man walked out of the kitchen with him and embraced Angie warmly. 'Always I say to Nikos that eventually he find a woman who is beautiful *and* clever. You are that woman.' He kissed her on both cheeks. 'You will visit us again soon.'

They drove home at a leisurely pace and Nikos uttered a long, fluent curse as he saw a black limousine parked at the front of the villa. 'It appears we have visitors.'

She watched as his knuckles whitened on the steering wheel. Obviously not very welcome visitors. 'What's wrong? Who is it?'

He switched off the engine, his handsome face an expressionless mask. 'It's my mother.' He ran a hand over his roughened jaw and for a moment she thought he might actually turn the car round and drive away from the villa. But, before he could move, the door opened and a tall, elegant woman walked down the steps.

Angie felt herself stiffen with embarrassment. For some reason, the reality of meeting Nikos's family hadn't entered her head. What would they think of this marriage? What would they think of *her*?

'Nikolaus!' The woman hurried towards the car but before she could reach them she was overtaken by a young girl who sprinted towards them, long dark hair flying around her shoulders.

'Nik!' She bounded towards the car and flung her arms round Nikos before he could extract himself from the driving seat. 'We wanted to surprise you.'

'You've certainly done that.' Nikos's tone was rough but there was warmth in his eyes as he stroked a hand over the girl's head.

'She was desperate to see you.' His mother had reached them and Nikos climbed out of the car and embraced his mother. 'Let's go inside.'

'Nik, even you can't be that rude!' The girl turned to Angie, her face glowing with excitement. 'I'm Ariadne; I'm Nik's sister. I want to know everything—'

Nikos's jaw hardened. 'Ariadne—'

'Well, you are such a dark horse!' Ariadne turned to him,

dark hair swinging around her face. 'I think you're never going to marry anyone, all my friends are living in hope, and then all of a sudden we hear that you've fallen in love and got married in England! How romantic is *that*?'

Not very, Angie thought painfully, wondering what the teenager would say if she knew the truth of their relationship. Aware of a swift exchange of looks between Nikos and his mother, Angie wondered just how much the older woman knew.

Did she know that this marriage was a sham?

Nikos introduced her formally and then they all made their way to the terrace that overlooked the pool and the beach and Maria, Nikos's housekeeper, served iced drinks.

After half an hour of polite conversation, Ariadne stripped off her jeans and her top and walked down the steps to the pool. Nikos followed and Angie was left alone with his mother.

Suddenly she felt impossibly shy. 'You must think this marriage is very sudden, Mrs Kyriacou,' she said in a strangled voice and was surprised when the older woman covered her hand with her own.

'Call me Eleni,' she said gently, 'and please don't feel awkward. I always knew that when Nikos finally fell in love he'd do it instantly and with no fuss and bother. It's part of the man he is. He knows his own mind. Always has.'

'Oh—well—'

'I'm just so relieved that everything has worked out.' She glanced towards the pool, watching with a benevolent smile as Nikos threw Ariadne into the water. 'For a while I was really worried about him—he sacrificed so much for us—'

Angie stared at her. Sacrifice wasn't a word she associated with Nikos. 'He did?'

Eleni gave a shudder and reached for her drink. 'I can hardly bear to think about it. There was this girl—' She took a sip of her drink. 'She was exceptionally beautiful and extremely young.'

Despite the heat of the day, Angie felt suddenly cold. Instinctively she knew who Eleni was talking about and she wanted to stop her. Wanted to warn her that the girl in question was her sister, but her mouth wouldn't move.

'Few men would have been able to resist her,' Eleni murmured sadly, the expression on her face wistful and tired. 'I don't blame anyone. But I was worried about Nikos.'

'I would think he's old enough to look after himself.' Her lips stiff, somehow Angie managed to formulate the words. 'Why shouldn't he have an affair with her?'

Eleni made a sympathetic noise and covered Angie's hand with her own. 'Now I've upset you and for no reason. It wasn't Nikos who had an affair with the girl—it was Aristotle. My husband.'

'Your husband?' Angie's voice cracked as she struggled to grasp the implication of those words.

'My husband isn't always wise when it comes to women. Several times during our marriage he's—' Eleni broke off and gave a wan smile, clearly finding the subject matter distressing. 'Never mind, you don't need the details. He always comes back to me and that's what counts, but this time was different. *She* was different. Cold. Calculating. She knew what she wanted. Marriage. Him. At any cost.'

Angie sat in perfect stillness, hardly able to breathe. 'Marriage? To your husband?'

'Aristotle was a fool, of course. He should have seen what sort of girl she was, but he didn't. She was scheming and greedy. I was so afraid. If it hadn't been for Nikos—' Her eyes were haunted and she took a sip of wine. 'I almost didn't tell him. I didn't want to worry him but when I discovered the diamond was missing I was afraid it was serious—'

'She stole the diamond?'

Eleni shook her head. 'It went missing and I was afraid that Aristotle had given it to her as a gift. The diamond has great significance within our family. Had my husband given it to his mistress then it would have meant only one thing—'

'That the relationship was serious?'

'That's right.' Eleni's smile was wan. 'Fortunately I was wrong about the jewel. The diamond was with Nikos all the time. Aristotle asked him to have the stone polished and the setting checked. Nikos's schedule is so packed it had taken him ages to sort it out and it was lying in his safe, forgotten!'

Angie felt like an impostor, sitting here, having this conversation without revealing her true relationship to the girl in question. *Without revealing what she knew about the diamond.* She understood now why Nikos had needed the necklace so urgently. 'So the girl's relationship with your husband wasn't serious?'

Eleni looked away. 'He hadn't given her the diamond and that meant a lot to me. I was worried that the relationship might be more than a fling but Nikos proved otherwise. He played the girl at her own game. Pretended to be attracted to her, wooed her away from his father. If nothing else, his success in that direction proved what Nikos had always believed—that she was never really interested in Aristotle, only in his money. She was more than happy to switch to Nikos. It helped me to know that she hadn't been left broken-hearted.'

Somehow, Angie made her lips form the question that was on her mind. 'Was she really that scheming?'

'Unfortunately, yes. And then she had that terrible accident. I'm sure Nikos has told you, although he hates to be reminded of it—he feels responsible, even though he wasn't there.'

In a daze of horror, Angie closed her fingers around the seat of the chair. 'What do you mean?'

'The day before she died, he'd told her that their relationship was over. She was upset and angry. She turned up at his house but he was at a meeting in his offices in town. The staff saw that she was drunk and called him but by the time he arrived at the house she was dead and the police were there.'

'She fell from the balcony.'

Eleni closed her eyes. 'Fortunately no blame attached to Nikos because he wasn't even there, but he just hated the scandal that erupted. As usual, he was desperate to protect Ariadne and me. He took all the flak. Aristotle's name wasn't even mentioned and it's all thanks to him.'

'Yes.' Angie's lips were stiff and her gaze slid to Nikos, who was lifting Ariadne out of the water and swinging her round.

'So now you understand why I so badly wanted him to find a nice girl. He's always been cynical about women—I suppose that comes from watching his father go from one affair to another. But after that girl died—'

Angie sat in frozen stillness, her stomach churning alarmingly. Nikos hadn't played a game with her sister. He'd been protecting his mother and his little sister. *From Tiffany.*

A vile, terrible sickness rose inside her.

'Are you all right?' Eleni glanced at her with concern in her eyes. 'You look very pale.'

'I have a headache.' Feeling dangerously lightheaded, Angie stood up suddenly and her chair scraped the terrace. 'If you'll excuse me, I think I need to lie down.'

'Of course. It's probably the sun. You have such lovely fair skin you must be careful not to burn.' Eleni reached out and caught her hand. 'I've been talking too much. I hope I haven't upset you.'

'No.' Angie managed a smile that she hoped was reassuring. 'I'm fine. Really.'

She hurried into the villa, took the stairs and just made it into their bathroom before she was violently sick.

'*Meu Dios*, what is wrong with you? You are ill?' A harsh male voice came from directly behind her and she gave a groan and sank on to the bathroom floor, her arms wrapped round her waist.

'Not now, Nikos—I need privacy.'

'You look as though you need a doctor.'

'I'm fine, really.'

'Fine doesn't run from the terrace as if being chased by a wild animal. Fine isn't being violently sick.' His tone grim, he reached down and lifted her, placing her gently on the seat in the corner of the bathroom. Then he held a towel under the tap and gently wiped her face and mouth. 'Lie down on the bed and I will call the doctor. Is it the heat? Were you outside without a hat?'

She shook her head, wondering why his sudden attentiveness should be so painful to bear. But she knew the answer to that, of course. She knew now that she was here under false pretences. She'd forced him into marriage as a punishment and yet she'd just discovered that he hadn't ever committed the crime of which she'd accused him.

No wonder he'd been so angry with her.

No wonder he'd shown such contempt towards Tiffany.

Cursing softly in Greek, he swung her into his arms and carried her through to the bedroom. Laying her carefully in the middle of the bed, he picked up the phone and barked a series of orders. Moments later there was a tap on the door and two of his staff entered, carrying trays loaded with iced drinks and assorted delicacies.

'You're probably not eating enough.' His voice was gruff as he poured her a cup of tea. 'Try one of these pastries. They're good.'

'I couldn't eat a thing. Honestly.' At that precise moment in time, she didn't think she'd ever be able to eat again. Her stomach was churning alarmingly and her head was beginning to throb.

He dismissed the staff with an impatient wave of his bronzed hand and sat down on the bed. His handsome features were serious. 'Tell me what is wrong.'

She felt numb with shock. 'Your mother—'

'My mother upset you?' His brows came together in a frown and she shook her head quickly.

'No. At least, yes, but it wasn't her fault.' Her eyes filled and she raised her head, plucking up courage to look at him. 'She told me, Nikos. She told me everything.'

CHAPTER TEN

He STARED at her for a long moment, his powerful body unnaturally still. 'What do you mean by "everything"?'

Angie swallowed. 'I mean that she told me that Tiffany had
an affair with your father.' She could hardly bring herself to
say the words. 'I had no idea.'

'No one knew. I made sure of it. My father's behaviour has
caused more than enough distress to this family in the past.
My mother and Ariadne didn't need more.'

'Why didn't you tell me?'

He shrugged, his expression cold and remote. 'Had you
known the truth, you would have gone to the press. The last
time my mother read the details of my father's infidelities in
her daily newspaper, she tried to take her own life. My sister,
my fourteen-year-old sister, found her mother lying on the
carpet in a pool of her own vomit, empty bottles of tablets by
her side, newspapers open at the pages that reported my
father's latest indiscretion. Unfortunately that particular girl
saw an alternative way to make money and supplied the press
with no end of sordid details, most of which were false.'

Angie closed her eyes at the vision his words created. So
that was why he hated the media. *Not because he was worried
about his own image.* 'Your mother tried to kill herself—'

'That's right. Her marriage to my father has been punctuated by misery but such a public humiliation was too much for her. You can see now, perhaps, why I wished to restore the diamond to my family with the minimum of fuss.'

She could see everything. And she felt *dreadful*. 'Whatever you may think of me, I wouldn't have gone to the press—'

'Wouldn't you?' He raised an eyebrow. 'The first time we met you talked about having read about me in newspapers. You clearly had no understanding of how destructive the media can be. And at the time you hated me enough to do anything—enough to force me into marriage. Why wouldn't you have sold your story to the media?'

'But if you'd told me the truth about Tiffany—'

'You would never have believed me. You'd made up your mind that I was an evil seducer who had set out to ruin your sister, and in a way you were right.' He stood up then and walked over to the window, keeping his back to her. 'It's true that I set out to take her away from my father. It's also true that I broke off the relationship and that she died falling from my balcony. The only thing that wasn't true was your assessment of her feelings for me. She was never in love with me. We never even spent a night together.'

Angie stared at him. 'What are you saying? That you never—'

'I'm saying that I never had sex with your sister. I had no wish to sleep with my father's ex-mistress.'

He hadn't slept with her sister.

It shouldn't have mattered but it *did*. She felt relieved but she knew that such a sentiment was entirely misplaced. 'Did she love your father?'

'What do you think?' He turned to face her and she looked away rather than meet the hard cynicism in his eyes.

'And I suppose she didn't love you either—'

SARAH MORGAN   159

'I think she loved the idea of the position and the money,' Nikos said wearily, 'but I have to admit I didn't know she was expecting marriage until you showed me that text. My intention was simply to draw her away from my father.'

'Oh, God, was she really that desperate?' Her voice cracked and she covered her face with her hands. 'It's *all* my fault.'

'How is it your fault?'

'I should have tried harder with her. I should have insisted that she change her lifestyle. I should have refused to let her push me away—'

'You would have had no influence over your sister.' His tone cold, he walked over to the table and poured himself a glass of water. 'Despite her young age, she was a hard, calculating woman, driven by greed and lacking in morals.'

Angie subdued her natural instinct to defend her sister. How could she defend the indefensible? *How could she defend someone she'd clearly never known?* 'She was young.' She swallowed painfully. 'Perhaps I could have influenced her if I'd tried harder.'

He gave a humourless laugh. 'I think not. Your sister made a career choice and no one was going to shift her from her chosen path.'

'What do you mean, "a career choice"?'

'To marry a rich man.' He drank the water and put the glass down on the tray with exaggerated care. 'Unfortunately for my family, she targeted my father. When we first met, you said that Tiffany should never have moved in the same circles as my family and in a way you were right. We never would have met her had she not made a determined effort. Before my father there was another man—a millionaire shrewder than my father. He refused to play the game she wanted so she then threw herself in my father's path and pursued him like the predator she was. She played the part of the vulnerable, innocent female extremely effectively. He didn't stand a chance.'

'Please—' Angie covered her ears with her hands, unable to listen to any more. 'Oh, God, I can't believe I'm hearing this. Why didn't you tell me this before? Why?'

'I've already told you. You would never have believed me. You would have gone straight to the press. And this time my mother might have succeeded.'

Her eyes met his and she knew that he was remembering all the times that he'd told her that he wasn't responsible for her sister's death, that he'd never intended to marry her. 'I wouldn't have gone to the press,' she whispered finally, 'but you're right that I wouldn't have believed you. I didn't know any of those things about her and I was upset. I loved her so much and I missed her and—' she closed her eyes and ran a hand over her face '—and I was angry. Too angry to listen. I didn't want to part with the jewel because she'd worn it. I couldn't bear the fact that you didn't seem to care.'

He nodded. 'I can understand that. But I was angry too. Angry that you always seemed to be excusing her behaviour. That you seemed to approve of the person she was.'

'I knew she was flighty and fun-loving. I didn't know her as a predator. I still can't—' Angie broke off and licked dry lips. 'Your mother has no idea who I am. It would shatter her if she found out that your father gave the jewel to Tiffany and she'd be horrified if she knew the truth of our marriage.'

'She isn't going to find out that my father gave your sister the jewel. She would attribute a false significance to an act that was nothing more than an impulsive, foolish gesture. As far as my mother is aware, the jewel has been safely in my keeping for the past six months and I am married to the bride of my choice.'

'But it's not true, is it?' Angie's voice was agonized as her brain sifted through the facts. 'I'm *not* the bride of your choice. We both know that I'm the last woman you would have chosen to marry. We're *totally* wrong for each other. And this isn't some stranger we're talking about who threatened the security of your family, this was my *sister*. I *have* to tell your mother the truth. I have to explain about Tiffany—apologise if I can—make amends—'

And yet how could she possibly make amends when she was part of the problem? When she was the reason that Nikos was now married to a woman he didn't love and never would?

There was a long throbbing silence while he stared at her. 'You will not raise the subject with my mother. To do so would reveal that my father gave the necklace to your sister and I won't allow you to cause her such unnecessary distress.'

Angie sank her head on to her hands. 'Why didn't you argue with me? What *possessed* you to agree to marry me? Nobody makes you do anything you don't want to do. You're ruthless, single-minded and totally focused on what you want. *Why did you say yes to me?*'

'I needed the jewel and I needed it quickly.'

'You could have used lawyers—'

'And that would have attracted the attention of the press, which was the one thing I had to avoid. I see no benefit at all in this line of conversation. The past cannot be changed however much we might wish that it could be.' He glanced at his watch. 'I need to join my mother and sister or they will start asking questions that I have no intention of answering. Do you promise me that you won't raise the matter of your relationship to Tiffany with my mother? When the time is right I will explain that you are her sister and that we met when I went to London to meet her family and offer condolences. It's the truth, after all.'

What could she say? She nodded silently, swamped by a

guilt so enormous that she couldn't think straight. 'If that's what you want.'

'It is. You look white and exhausted.' He strode towards the door. 'Go to bed. I'll have dinner sent up on a tray and I'll try and persuade my family that they really don't want to spend the night here.'

'Wait—' Feeling wrung out and suddenly frantic to make it up to him in some way, she slid off the bed and walked across to him. 'We have to be able to do something to retrieve the situation. I'll give you a divorce.'

He stared down at her, a muscle flickering in his lean jaw. 'It is as I said before. Unfortunately my lawyers are the best. The agreement we both signed is watertight. Whether you like it or not, we are married, *agape mou*, for better or for worse, for the period of two years, just as you stipulated. To the outside world we are now married and I, for one, have no desire to see yet more scandal and speculation attached to my family.' His eyes held hers and she shifted uncomfortably.

This was the part where she was supposed to say that he could see other women. But she couldn't bring herself to say the words and suddenly she knew why.

She couldn't say the words because she didn't *want* him to see other women.

Not because she wanted to punish him, but because she loved him.

She really, really loved him.

The sudden knowledge pinned her to the spot and she didn't utter a word as he gave her a searching, slightly impatient look and then left the room, closing the door behind him, leaving her to wallow in the knowledge that she'd never really known anything about her sister.

And neither had she known anything about herself.

Until now.

* * *

She spent a sleepless night alone in their room, wondering where Nikos was sleeping. *Wondering what he was thinking.* Now that she knew the truth about Tiffany, she felt deeply ashamed and hideously guilty. Her beliefs about him and her beliefs about herself and her sister had been brutally destroyed, leaving her with no safe foundations on which to build a future.

She'd failed Tiffany and she'd treated Nikos incredibly badly.

Lost in contemplation of how she might begin to right some of the wrongs that her family had done him, it took a few moments for her to realise that he was standing by the bed. One glance at his unshaven jaw and tired eyes told her that wherever he'd spent the night, it hadn't been anywhere comfortable.

'I came to apologise for my behaviour last night.'

She stared at him blankly. 'Your behaviour? What do you have to apologise for?'

'I laid all the blame at your sister's door but the truth was that my father was also responsible for what happened.' His broad shoulders rigid with tension, he cursed softly and paced across the room, keeping his back to her. 'My father has always had a problem with fidelity. Your sister was not his first affair.'

'What my sister did was very wrong.'

'But she had targeted other men before and they had refused her. Seen her for what she was.' He turned to face her. 'My father could have done the same.'

Confronted by this alien picture of her sister, Angie tried not to flinch. 'You have nothing to apologise for. I'm the one who should be apologizing, both for Tiffany and myself.'

He gave a faint smile and dragged a hand through his hair. 'Apologising is a new experience for me and I'm not sure that I'm enjoying it, so why don't we both agree just to forget the past behaviour of our various relatives and move on from here?'

Move on? How could they possibly move on when she'd forced him into a marriage that was abhorrent to him?

She gave a weak smile. 'Of course.'

He stared at her for a moment as if there was something else he wanted to say and then he gave a soft curse and glanced towards the door. 'I have to go. I have a meeting in Athens and my pilot is waiting.'

'Of course.' Couldn't she think of something more original to say? They'd been getting on well, but suddenly her brain couldn't move past the fact that he was only in this marriage because of her. 'Have a good day.'

He hesitated a moment longer and then gave her a brief nod and left the room.

Angie flopped back against the pillow, a feeling of despair mingling with guilt. It didn't matter how she looked at things, there was no escaping the fact that she wasn't the wife he would have chosen.

He returned later that evening and they ate dinner on the terrace overlooking the private beach. The night was warm and candles flickered on the table between them, creating an air of intimacy that she found almost painful.

'Tell me about your sister.' He topped up her wineglass.

'You don't want to talk about her.'

'Actually, I do.' He leaned back in his chair, one dark brow lifted in a silent prompt and she curled her fingers round the wineglass to give her the courage she needed to talk.

'I was eight when she was born and I fell in love with her on sight. It was like having a real, live doll. She was so beautiful. And all mine.'

'All yours?'

Angie hesitated. 'My mother wasn't terribly keen on babies. To be honest, I'm not sure she would have had children at all if the choice had been hers. She—' She broke off, feeling suddenly disloyal towards her mother. 'She was quite busy with other things, so I looked after Tiffany.'

'You?' He frowned. 'You were eight years old.'

'I was a very mature eight-year-old,' Angie said quickly, 'and I loved looking after her. She was adorable. All blonde curls and smiles. She used to climb into my bed at night and sleep curled up against me. She was *so* sweet and warm and I loved it.' Feeling a lump growing in her throat, she took a large sip of wine, wishing that Nikos would stop looking at her in that curiously intent way.

'So you're saying that you virtually brought your sister up?'

She put the glass down on the table. 'Yes. Until she was seven. And then Mum— Well, I suppose she suddenly discovered she liked having a real little girl.' She gave a painful smile. 'I was always a bit of a disappointment to her in that way, as you know. I preferred books to dressing up and I was quiet and painfully shy. Tiffany was different in every way. Her favourite colour was pink and she loved everything girly.'

He studied her face. 'So your mother suddenly took over the responsibility for parenting.'

'Yes.'

'And you were so lonely that you spent even more time with your books,' he said softly and she glanced at him, startled.

'Well, I—' She met his gaze and then dropped her eyes, wondering why she'd ever thought he wasn't astute about people's feelings. 'Yes, I was lonely. And I missed Tiffany. We'd had such a special bond.' She took a deep breath and forced herself to admit something that she'd been denying for years. 'I suppose, if I'm honest, I carried on seeing Tiffany as that sweet little girl. I saw the change in her, of course. She loved going to parties and all she cared about was dressing up and flirting, but I still thought she was the same good person. I think what happened with my father affected her deeply.'

'He lost his money?'

'Everything. He had several affairs, very public ones, and he spent large sums of money.' She toyed with the food on her plate. 'I suppose he wanted to impress women. Unfortunately his business was already in trouble.'

'And your mother and Tiffany lost a lifestyle they'd come to enjoy.'

'Yes.' It was painful admitting something so shallow. 'I'd bought myself a little flat which I loved but in the end I rented it out and moved back home so that I could help Mum financially. But the biggest problem was Tiffany. She really resented the fact that Dad had spent all his money on these women. She kept saying that she was going to go out and—' She broke off, pink with embarrassment and he finished her sentence, his tone cool.

'—she was going to go out and do the same to some other guy.'

'It wasn't really her fault,' Angie said quickly. 'Mum kept telling her that she was beautiful enough to attract a really rich man, so Tiffany grew up with that expectation.' She put down her fork and rubbed her forehead with shaking fingers. 'It sounds so awful.'

'There are plenty of women out there who think the same way.'

She looked at him. 'Is that why you've never married?'

'I've never married because I've never met a woman I wanted to spend more than five minutes with.' He gave a faint smile of self-mockery. 'I have an *extremely* short attention span. And, despite what you think of me, I wouldn't want to cause a woman the pain that my father caused my mother.'

'Did she never think of leaving him?'

'She loves him,' Nikos said, 'and love makes people do foolish things.'

'Yes.' She could easily understand that because now she was in love she was tempted to do no end of foolish things, including making a wild declaration about her feelings for him.

She almost laughed aloud at the thought of his reaction. What would he say if he knew the truth of how she felt about him?

He'd laugh and he'd be horrified. And he'd also pity her for believing that she could ever be the sort of woman he'd willingly select as his wife.

No. She lifted her glass to her lips and stayed silent. There was no way she was going to complicate things further by confessing her true feelings.

They finished dinner, lingered over coffee and then finally went up to bed.

'I have an early meeting,' Nikos said in a cool tone, removing his shirt in a swift decisive movement. 'I'll sleep next door so that I don't wake you.'

He wanted to sleep next door?

Everything had changed, she thought miserably. The fragile truce that had existed between them had been shattered by her discovery of the truth.

She wanted to stop him leaving the room. She wanted to tell him that she was only too happy to spend the entire night awake as long as she was with him, but she knew that he didn't want to hear that.

He'd suddenly realised that this marriage needn't have happened and he clearly wanted to stay as far away from her as possible.

She gave a miserable nod. 'Fine. I'll see you tomorrow.'

Angie spent her second night without sleep, her brain playing with the problem.

She wasn't the woman he would have chosen but he was

stuck with her, so the least she could do was try and make things easier for him.

It was still early when she stood up and padded into the bathroom, scraping her hair out of her eyes and staring at her reflection in the mirror.

It wasn't all bad, she told herself firmly. He always said that he liked her eyes and surely a man couldn't fake the degree of sexual interest he'd shown towards her? All right, so last night he'd left the room with an unflattering degree of haste, but that didn't mean that she couldn't tempt him back.

He liked confident women, didn't he?

So, it was up to her to show him that she'd grown more confident.

And she had, she reminded herself, turning sideways and looking at her profile.

Experimenting with her new wardrobe had been fun and she was starting to learn what suited her and what didn't.

And their relationship didn't have to be about looks and sex. She was cleverer than his previous girlfriends and he was *definitely* finding her useful in some of his meetings.

She gave a sigh and let her hair fall back over her face. What was the use of pretending? A man like Nikos wasn't interested in whether a woman was clever or not. A man like Nikos didn't need a woman who was going to be useful in meetings; he had an entire payroll of staff for that purpose. He needed a woman to occupy him in a different way. He needed a confident, beautiful, sexual woman.

And that wasn't her. Not really. She was improving, that was true, but she was still nothing like the women he usually dated.

She chewed her lip and sank down on the edge of the bath, deep in thought. She'd already discovered that she enjoyed clothes and socialising far more than she would ever have thought possible. His friends and colleagues seemed to find her more than acceptable. The only area that needed work was the bedroom. She was painfully aware of her lack of experience in that area. That he was always the one in control.

But was it really so hard for her to take the initiative?

She didn't know anything about seducing men, but so far she'd done nothing to intentionally attract him and he'd had no trouble having sex with her, so presumably if she made an effort—

Glancing at her watch, she saw she had the whole day ahead of her, which was just as well, she mused as she stared in the mirror at her unruly, tangled hair, because she was going to need every second if she was going to transform herself into the sort of woman that Nikos usually had on his arm.

Nikos sprang out of the helicopter, his mind still on the meeting he'd just left.

Was it his imagination, or was he finding it harder and harder to concentrate these days?

He strode across the lawn and up the steps of the villa and then stopped dead, staring in amazement at the woman standing in front of him. It took several moments for him to realise that it was Angie.

'What have you done to yourself?' He saw the colour rise into her cheeks and cursed himself for being so tactless. 'I mean, you look great, of course. Just not like you.'

Her amazing hair had been styled and blown straight and now slithered over her shoulders, *her bare, creamy shoulders*, in a silken curtain that gleamed and shone in the strong Greek sunlight. Her elegant silk dress was short enough to remind him that she had legs that went on for ever and her slender arms were bare.

She gave a slightly shy smile. 'Actually this is me. Just a different part of me, I suppose. I've discovered that I really like dressing up. I like the clothes you bought me. I know you only bought them for me because you didn't want me to embarrass you in public,' she said quickly, 'but I'm really enjoying them. Thank you.'

Aware that some sort of response was required, he struggled to drag his eyes away from the tempting dip of her cleavage. 'You look great.'

'Let's go upstairs.' Her tone was slightly husky and Nikos lifted a hand to his collar and loosened his tie with a jerk.

'It's extremely *hot* today—'

She smiled and held out a hand. 'It's cooler inside.'

Overcome by a painful attack of lust, Nikos followed her upstairs to their bedroom, reminding himself that she hadn't really chosen to be in this relationship and sex was probably no longer a part of it.

But it was impossible not to think about sex when she was looking at him with those amazing blue eyes.

Was he allowed to kiss her?

Confused about how to behave with a woman for the first time in his life, Nikos pushed the bedroom door shut and watched with a sense of wary anticipation as she strolled towards him and lifted her hands to the buttons of his shirt.

'Did you have a stressful day?' Her voice was smoky and feminine and he felt his body's instant and very powerful reaction.

'Yes.'

'Good.' She smiled and slid the shirt from his shoulders, her fingers sliding slowly over his heated flesh. 'Because I know you always need to relax when you're stressed.'

He stared down at her. 'Angelina, *agape mou*, you can't—'

'Why can't I? You're the one who taught me to enjoy sex, Nikos, so if you don't like the person I am then you have only yourself to blame.'

At a loss for words for the first time in his life, Nikos was struggling to formulate a coherent sentence when he felt her fingers release the button of his trousers and slide them down to the floor.

'Angelina—' He groaned her name, sure that there was some sort of conversation that they should be having but unable to formulate his thoughts into any sort of logical order.

He struggled for control but suddenly realised that he was entirely naked and she was now on her knees in front of him.

'I've never actually done this before,' she murmured huskily as her mouth trailed over his abdomen and lower still to his straining erection, 'so you're going to have to tell me if I do anything wrong.'

Wrong?

He tried to say something but at that moment her soft, wet mouth slid over his throbbing shaft and he gritted his teeth and closed his eyes. Close to losing control, he tried to focus his mind on something serious but her fingers and her tongue were everywhere and the pressure inside his body built to dangerous levels.

'Angelina—' Speaking was difficult but he forced his eyes open and then wished he hadn't because the look in her eyes was all woman, *all seductive, sexy woman*, and he knew that there was no hope of gaining any sort of control.

Her tongue and fingers tortured him with pleasure. 'Does it feel good, Nikos?' She removed her mouth from him just long enough to speak and then took him in her mouth again and he felt the agonising ache in his loins build to unbearable levels.

'Angelina, you have to—you can't—' And then his entire world exploded in a climax so intense that for a moment the world around him went black. The powerful throb of his release went on and on and all the time he was aware of her soft, clever mouth touching him.

Finally, just when he was beginning to wonder whether he'd ever feel normal again, his body calmed and he sagged against the door with his eyes closed.

He felt her move. Felt her mouth press a gentle kiss against his chest and then she was tugging at his hand, leading him to the bed.

Still recovering from what could only be described as an explosive experience and only too happy to lie down, Nikos sprawled on the covers with his eyes closed.

'Just how stressful was your day?' She straddled him and slid her hands up his chest before lowering her mouth to his. Her silken hair fell forward, tickling his bare skin, and he lifted a hand and brushed it away from her face, trying to find the energy to speak.

'That was amazing—'

'It isn't finished yet.'

He wasn't sure which was more erotic. The look in her eyes, the sound of her voice or the feel of her body over his. 'I need some recovery time—'

'That's fine by me. You just lie there and I'll do all the work.'

Still dazed after the most explosive orgasm of his life, he stared up at her in disbelief. 'What's happened to you?'

'You happened to me,' she said, sliding a hand over his hard abdomen and touching him intimately. 'You changed me from Angie to Angelina. You showed me a different part of myself and I really, *really* like it.' She positioned herself above him and slowly lowered her hips.

He gave a groan of disbelief and slid his hands over her silken flesh, trying to hold her still—trying to take some of the control back. 'I think I like it too, but you have to stop moving for a minute. Just for a minute—'

'I'm not sure that I can.' She leaned forward and caught his lower lip between her teeth, biting gently. 'I've been thinking about you since you left this morning, you see. And it's been a *very* long day.'

'Tell me about it.' Her tight, velvety warmth gripped him and his eyes closed. The smooth, seductive movement of her hips drove him to the point of desperation and suddenly he gave a soft curse and flipped her on to her back, coming down on top of her in a fluid, confident movement. 'Enough.'

'Enough?' Her eyes went wide and he gave a satisfied smile that was totally masculine.

'Enough of being teased. Now I'm the one in control.' He slid a hand under her bottom, raised her and his powerful thrust brought a gasp of ecstasy to her lips.

'Oh—yes—Nikos—'

'You feel *so* good—' He brought his mouth down on hers and kissed her deeply, the movement of his tongue mimicking the intimate thrust of his body and almost immediately he felt her tremble and felt her body tighten around his. The ripples of her orgasm triggered his own and he swallowed her cries and held her tightly as they both flung themselves over the edge into an abyss of sexual pleasure.

It was fine, Angie told herself a week later as she dressed for the formal dinner they were attending. He might not love her but he *definitely* had a good time in bed and wasn't ashamed to be seen with her in public. It wasn't such a bad marriage.

She saw him enter the bedroom behind her and paused in the process of fastening an earring. 'Do we have to go out?'

He frowned as he reached for his jacket. 'You have no reason to feel shy. You are an intelligent woman and you speak fluent Greek. You are a match for any social situation.'

'Thank you, although that wasn't really what I meant.' She blushed at the unexpected compliment. 'I just thought it would be nice if we could stay in.'

'We have "stayed in" for the last week,' he drawled, humour lighting his dark eyes. 'And now I need to go out for a rest.'

She smiled. 'Tired, Nikos?'

'You are insatiable. I had no idea what it would be like to be married to a sex maniac.'

She laughed. 'You taught me everything I know.'

'And make sure it stays that way.' He hauled her to her feet and brought his mouth down on hers in a possessive kiss. 'Dimitri will be there tonight. If you have to talk to him then do so from a distance of at least two metres.'

She knew he didn't love her but surely the fact that he didn't want her to flirt with other men suggested that he must care a bit?

The ballroom of the exclusive hotel was crowded with people and Angie was surprised and more than a little disturbed to spot Nikos's mother across the room.

'She is patron of the charity,' Nikos said smoothly, intercepting her worried glance. 'Most of Athens society is here. This dinner is an annual event. Very boring. Don't worry. Just behave naturally. We'll leave as soon as I've spoken to the people I came to see.'

Throughout dinner Angie chatted to the man on her right, a lawyer based in Athens, but she was all too aware of Nikos seated right beside her, talking to a slender blonde.

He had every right to enjoy another woman's company, she reminded herself, waiting until the meal finally ended and excusing herself so that she could breathe in some fresh air.

She walked on to the terrace and down on to the lawn and sat by the edge of a bubbling fountain.

Lost in thought it took a moment for her to realise that two people were having a conversation on the terrace above her, And that those two people were Nikos and his mother.

Knowing instinctively that she wasn't going to like what she heard, Angie tried to stand up and declare her presence but her legs wouldn't hold her and her tongue wouldn't move. She sat in stillness, frozen to the spot in horrified anticipation.

They spoke in Greek but Angie had no trouble understanding what they were saying.

'She's the sister?'

'Older sister.'

'There's only one reason why you would have married a woman like that. Someone related to that terrible girl. Money. She's blackmailed you, hasn't she?' Eleni's voice cracked. 'She's threatened to go to the press or something like that. Something worse—'

'I love Angelina. And I don't want her sister discussed again.'

At that point there were more voices on the terrace and Angie assumed that Nikos and his mother had found a more peaceful place to continue their conversation.

She sat for a moment feeling numb. How had his mother referred to her?

A woman like that.

And she wasn't even in a position to deny the charges made against her. She *had* blackmailed Nikos. Not for money, that was true, but for the jewel, which was possibly even worse. He'd sacrificed himself in order to protect his family. He was lying about loving her to spare his mother's feelings. He was a man of honour, whereas she—

She was just someone who *never* should have been with him.

Tiffany had almost destroyed his family.

How had she ever been foolish enough to think that dressing up and showing that she enjoyed sex would be enough for him? He didn't love her and he never would. He was just saying that to soften his mother's opinion of her. And it was crazy for the two of them to stay together. She'd created this situation but she could also undo it. She could set him free. She should set him free.

But how, when she loved him so much?

Her eyes filled as she contemplated exactly what setting him free would mean.

In an agony of indecision, she sat for a moment, battling with a powerful urge to ignore the honest, responsible side of her nature. They were legally bound for the next two years. He had to stay with her. She could remain as his wife and hope in time he'd fall in love with her. She could—

She could stop kidding herself.

With an impatient sigh, she stood up and took a deep breath, reminding herself of her personal values. She'd done wrong, but she could put it right. Nikos would never fall in love, especially not with a woman like her, and she needed to set him free.

No matter what the cost to her, she was going to do that.

She'd return to England, she decided. She'd ask the solicitor to draw up a document that would renounce all her rights to the Brandizi diamond.

She'd return home. But not to her old life. She loved her job but she was no longer prepared to live with her mother, nor was she willing to consider an evening at a lecture the be all and end all of her social life.

It wouldn't be right to take the clothes that Nikos had given her but that didn't stop her going on her own shopping spree. She'd revamp her wardrobe and use her new found confidence to get out and enjoy life. She just wasn't the old Angie any more. For the first time in her life she felt different.

She straightened her shoulders and brushed away tears that she hadn't even been aware of shedding. Yes, she was in love with Nikos. Yes, it was going to be painful and difficult to live without him. But she'd learn in the same way that she'd learned everything else.

She wasn't Angie any more—she was Angelina.

And the next thing she'd have to learn was how to live without him.

CHAPTER ELEVEN

'I CAN'T believe the change in you. You look so different. And I can't believe you're seriously moving to Greece.'

'Why not? Greek history has always been my passion. I can't think why I didn't do it before.' Angie staggered under the weight of a box of books that she was carrying to the attic. 'This is the last one and then I need to get ready, Mum. I'm going out tonight.'

Her mother gave a sniff. 'Another lecture at the museum with one of those boring professor types you insist on hanging around with, I suppose.'

'No, actually.' Angie heaved the last of the boxes up the ladder and pushed it into the attic. 'I'm going to the opening night of that new play at the Aldwych.' On her own, but her mother didn't need to know that.

Since she'd returned from Crete and started going out more, she'd had plenty of offers from men, but she'd found it impossible to say yes to any of them. Until her divorce was finalised she wasn't going to date anyone and anyway, she thought wistfully as she stacked the box on top of the others, none of the men were Nikos. He put all other men into the shade.

'Well, if you're harbouring romantic thoughts about that billionaire of yours, you're wasting your time. If you'd wanted

to hang on to him then you never should have returned his
jewel.' Her mother folded her arms. 'A man like him would
never have been happy with someone like you.'

Angie negotiated the ladder and then turned and faced her
mother. 'The jewel belonged to him, which is why I returned
it. And I think, in different circumstances, a man like him could
be extremely happy with a woman like me. Unfortunately for
both of us, Tiffany's behaviour almost destroyed his family.
That will always be between us. It was my choice to leave and
I have no intention of seeking to resume our relationship.'

Her mother frowned. 'You've got plenty to say for yourself
all of a sudden. And you look different. Posh. What's the
point in wearing lip gloss when he isn't even here to see it?'

'I like wearing lip gloss and I'm not doing it for him, I'm
doing it for me.' Angie walked into the living room and
scooped up the last of her things. 'It's who I am.'

'Well, I must admit you look better, although you'll never
hold a candle to Tiffany, of course.'

'And I wouldn't want to. I'm me, Mum. And I'm proud to
be me. This is who I am.' She reached out and picked up the
photograph of Tiffany as a two-year-old, innocence shining out
of her eyes. 'I'm taking this because this is how I think of her
and it's how I want to remember her.' *Not as a home-wrecker.*

Her mother looked taken aback. 'Well, of course, you've
always been the clever one, but Tiffany—'

'Tiffany's dead, Mum. I miss her and always will. But now
we need to get on with our lives.' Angie glanced at her watch.
'I'll say goodbye now because you're going next door for
supper and I'm going straight to the airport from the theatre.
As soon as I'm settled in Greece, I'll send you my address
and you can come and stay.'

'This is crazy.' Her mother frowned. 'You haven't even
found a job.'

'I have excellent qualifications and I speak fluent Greek. I'll find a job when I'm ready. To begin with I'm actually thinking of working as a volunteer on an archaeological dig.'

'A volunteer? Why would you want to do a thing like that?' Her mother couldn't hide her distaste. 'I will never understand you, Angelina.'

Angie slid her bag on to her shoulder. 'No, Mum,' she said quietly, 'I don't think you will. But it doesn't matter. I'm used to it now and I like who I am. I'm proud of who I am. Take care of yourself.'

She enjoyed the play, absorbed by the characters and the quality of the writing, and then finally it was over and she spilled out on to the damp London street with the rest of the crowd, all eager to make their way onto their next destination. Restaurants. Home.

Greece.

For a moment her heart ached and she felt a shaft of pain that came close to agony. Would it ever become easier? *Would she ever be able to forget him?*

Refusing to allow herself to become morose, she raised a hand to a passing taxi, but before the driver could stop and pick her up a long black limousine purred to a halt next to the kerb.

A door opened and Nikos stepped out.

For a moment she just stared at him stupidly. Was it really him or was her mind playing tricks? And then she noticed that the women spilling out of the theatre were gaping in admiration. Only Nikos attracted that sort of attention from the female sex.

What was he doing here?

Her heart leaped in crazy excitement and then she used logic to rein in her entirely foolish assumption that he'd come to see her.

Of course he hadn't come to see her.

Nikos ran an international business. He travelled all over the world.

He was here to close some deal or other.

Suddenly she wished that his deal had been in Brazil or somewhere equally distant. She wasn't sure she could survive seeing him so soon after forcing herself to leave.

She needed more time.

She'd spent a month trying to convince herself that she could live her life without him and suddenly, seeing him standing there, her confidence drained away.

How could she live without him, when not being with him felt like only half a life?

'What are you doing here, Nikos?' She managed what she hoped was a casual smile. 'More business meetings?'

'I'm concluding a very important deal.'

She nodded. Of course he was. 'I hope it went well for you.'

'Negotiations are only just beginning.' He seemed unusually tense and she glanced over his shoulder to see if she could spot another taxi.

She had to get away before she broke down and embarrassed him. 'I'm sure you'll achieve the outcome you want.'

'I'm banking on it. Get in the car, Angelina.'

'Sorry?' Her gaze swivelled to his and there was something in his eyes that made her heart stumble in her chest. 'I can't go anywhere with you. My flight leaves in two hours. I have hardly any time to get to the airport and the roads will be awful on a rainy night like this.'

'I'll take you to the airport.' He closed his strong fingers round her wrist and guided her to the car without giving her time to argue. He leaned forward, delivered instructions to the driver and then activated the screen that guaranteed them privacy. 'Where are you going, Angelina?'

Being in such a confined space with him was torture. She wanted to sink her hands into his thick, glossy hair and press her lips to his firm, sensuous mouth. 'I'm going to Greece.' Why not tell him the truth?

'You loved my country.'

At any other time his smug expression would have made her smile. Now it just made her sad but she hid her feelings carefully. 'Of course. I can't think why I didn't go there before. To start with it's just going to be an extended holiday; I'm volunteering on a dig. But I hope to find more permanent work eventually.'

The car was nosing its way through the crowded London streets, tyres hissing on the wet roads as it gradually ate up the miles. Eventually they drove on to the motorway that led to the airport.

'Why did you leave Crete without saying goodbye?'

She closed her eyes briefly and then turned her head to stare out of the window, afraid that her eyes would reveal too much. 'It seemed like the right thing to do.'

'I received the documents from your lawyer.'

'Good. You're basically a free man.'

'Unfortunately not.' His tone held none of its usual smooth confidence and she glanced towards him with a frown.

'There was something wrong with the documents?'

'Everything was wrong with them.'

'I didn't realise. The lawyer assured me that there was no impediment to divorce. He checked every angle.'

His eyes lingered on hers. 'He missed one extremely important factor.'

Her heart sank. She'd tried so hard to make sure nothing could go wrong. 'What? What did he miss?'

'He missed the fact that I'm in love with you. And that makes divorce impossible.'

She sat still, shock holding her immobile. 'Sorry?'

'I love you. And I won't let you divorce me because I'm sure that you love me too.' He moved closer to her in a lithe, athletic movement and his hand slid into her hair. 'You left because you overheard a conversation between me and my mother, isn't that right?'

'I—she—' Angie felt the brush of his fingers against the nape of her neck and the sudden sprint of her heart. 'What makes you say that?'

'Because it was the only possible explanation for your behaviour. Before the dinner we shared incredible mind-blowing sex. Everything was amazing. And then on the way home in the car you were silent. The next morning you were gone.'

She swallowed. 'There just didn't seem any point in waiting two years to do something that we could do immediately. You deserve to be allowed to get on with your life. It seemed to me that fewer people would be hurt that way. Including your mother.'

'I'm not interested in my mother,' he said quietly, lifting a hand and trailing his fingers down her cheek. 'Nor am I interested in your mother or your sister. In fact, at this present moment, I'm not interested in anyone but you. And I'm here because I agree that it's important to get on with my life. And my life is going to include you.'

She forced herself to draw back slightly. 'Nikos—'

'When I first met you in London I was furiously angry with your whole family and your apparent defence of your sister's appalling behaviour offended me greatly.'

'She behaved terribly,' Angie whispered, 'but she was still my sister.'

'And your loyalty to her does you credit, *agape mou*. At the time, my entire focus was on returning the diamond to my mother.'

'I understand that now. You must have been very worried about her.'

'She has had a great deal to endure but she is a strong woman and my father has learned an important lesson. We are doing it again—' with a low groan of frustration, he buried his face in her neck and kissed her '—talking about our families when all I want to do is talk about *us*.'

'There is no "us", Nikos.' She tried to pull away from him, unable to think clearly when he was so close. 'I behaved terribly, forcing you to marry me. But I was angry and I thought you were incredibly arrogant.'

'I *was* incredibly arrogant,' he murmured, his mouth trailing over the curve of her jaw towards her lips, 'and I didn't have to marry you. I could have said no. I could have called my lawyers. But I was already fascinated by you.'

She gave a soft gasp as his tongue teased the corner of her mouth. 'That's not true. You thought I was plain.'

'I never thought you were plain,' he muttered against her mouth. 'I noticed your incredible eyes on the first day we met, then I saw your hair loose and the first time I discovered your legs—' He stopped talking for several long minutes while he kissed her with disturbing thoroughness. When he finally lifted his head she was breathless.

'You said I had an unfortunate personality,' she gasped. 'Being seen with me was embarrassing.'

'I haven't met that many women who answer me back and are capable of holding a conversation about classical Greek pottery in my native tongue. It took a while for me to adjust to the fact that you are highly intelligent but I've done it,' he assured her hastily, 'and I find it a real turn-on. I'm incredibly proud of you.'

'You never would have married me if it hadn't been for my sister.'

'Then that's something that I will always be grateful to her for.' He looked out of the window and she suddenly realised that the car had stopped.

'This isn't Heathrow.'

'No. But my plane is here and I'm hoping that you'll fly back to Crete with me. If you want to volunteer on a dig, then that's fine and if you want to stay at home and have my babies then that's fine too. You can do whatever makes you happy.'

She stared at him, wondering if she'd heard correctly. 'Have your babies?'

'Of course. I am Greek and we love children.' He shrugged his broad shoulders and then reached inside his jacket and withdrew a box. 'We have come full circle because I am going to give you this.' He opened the box and she looked down and gave a soft gasp.

'It's the Brandizi diamond.'

'Given by the eldest son to the woman of his heart. And that's you, *agape mou*. Will you accept the diamond? Will you marry me?'

Her hand shaking slightly, she reached down and picked up the beautiful necklace. 'I couldn't bear to give this back because she'd worn it.'

'Then wear it now and remember the good in your sister,' he said softly, 'and know that I love you.'

The stone sparkled and shone in the semi-darkness. 'If my sister hadn't been wearing this necklace, we probably never would have met.'

'Then perhaps it was fate.' His voice was husky as he took the necklace from her fingers and fastened it around her neck. 'It suits you.'

'I'm scared to wear something so valuable.'

He smiled. 'There are two bodyguards in the front of the car and they are both armed, but the true value of this necklace lies in the sentiment behind the gift, not in the stone itself.' His smile faded. 'I never thought I would find a woman I wanted to give it to. I treated you so badly, *agape mou*. Can you forgive me?'

'What is there to forgive?'

He took a deep breath. 'I was hard and cold and very unapproachable. You were impossibly shy in the bedroom but I refused to allow you to hide.'

'And I'm grateful for that.' Her voice was soft. 'You showed me a part of myself that I hadn't even known existed. You made me feel beautiful for the first time in my life. You gave me a confidence that I'd only ever had in my professional life. You taught me to like who I am and that's a gift beyond price.'

'You don't regret what happened between us?'

'How can you possibly think that I'd regret anything so perfect? I love you too, Nikos. You're right about that.'

He took her face in his hands. 'And you'll come back to Greece with me?'

'Of course.' She smiled and turned her head so that her lips brushed his hand. 'It's where I belong. With you. For ever.'

REQUEST YOUR FREE BOOKS!

2 FREE NOVELS
PLUS 2
FREE GIFTS!

YES! Please send me 2 FREE Harlequin Presents® novels and my 2 FREE gifts. After receiving them, if I don't wish to receive any more books, I can return the shipping statement marked "cancel." If I don't cancel, I will receive 6 brand-new novels every month and be billed just $3.80 per book in the U.S., or $4.47 per book in Canada, plus 25¢ shipping and handling per book and applicable taxes, if any*. That's a savings of close to 15% off the cover price! I understand that accepting the 2 free books and gifts places me under no obligation to buy anything. I can always return a shipment and cancel at any time. Even if I never buy another book from Harlequin, the two free books and gifts are mine to keep forever.

106 HDN EEXK   306 HDN EEXV

Name _____ (PLEASE PRINT) _____

Address _____ Apt. # _____

City _____ State/Prov. _____ Zip/Postal Code _____

Signature (if under 18, a parent or guardian must sign) _____

Mail to the Harlequin Reader Service®:

IN U.S.A.
P.O. Box 1867
Buffalo, NY
14240-1867

IN CANADA
P.O. Box 609
Fort Erie, Ontario
L2A 5X3

Not valid to current Harlequin Presents subscribers.

Want to try two free books from another line?
Call 1-800-873-8635 or visit www.morefreebooks.com.

* Terms and prices subject to change without notice. NY residents add applicable sales tax. Canadian residents will be charged applicable provincial taxes and GST. This offer is limited to one order per household. All orders subject to approval. Credit or debit balances in a customer's account(s) may be offset by any other outstanding balance owed by or to the customer. Please allow 4 to 6 weeks for delivery.

HP06

If you love strong, commanding men—
you'll love this miniseries…

Men who can't be tamed...or so they think!

THE SICILIAN'S
MARRIAGE ARRANGEMENT
by Lucy Monroe

Hope is overjoyed when sexy Sicilian tycoon Luciano
proposes marriage. Hope is completely in love with
her gorgeous husband—until Luciano confesses
he had had no choice but to wed her....

On sale in February…buy yours today!

Brought to you by your favorite Harlequin Presents authors!